nickelodeon

降去神通

AVATAR
THE LAST AIRBENDER.

Published in the United States by Random House Children's Books, a division of Penguin Random House LLC, 1745 Broadway, New York, NY, 10019, and in Canada by Penguin Random House Canada Limited, Toronto.

ISBN 978-0-593-56941-2

rhcbooks.com

Printed in the United States of America
10 9 8 7 6 5 4 3 2 1

nickelodeon

降世神通

AVATAR
THE LAST AIRBENDER.

THE POWER OF TOPH

RANDOM HOUSE 🏠 NEW YORK

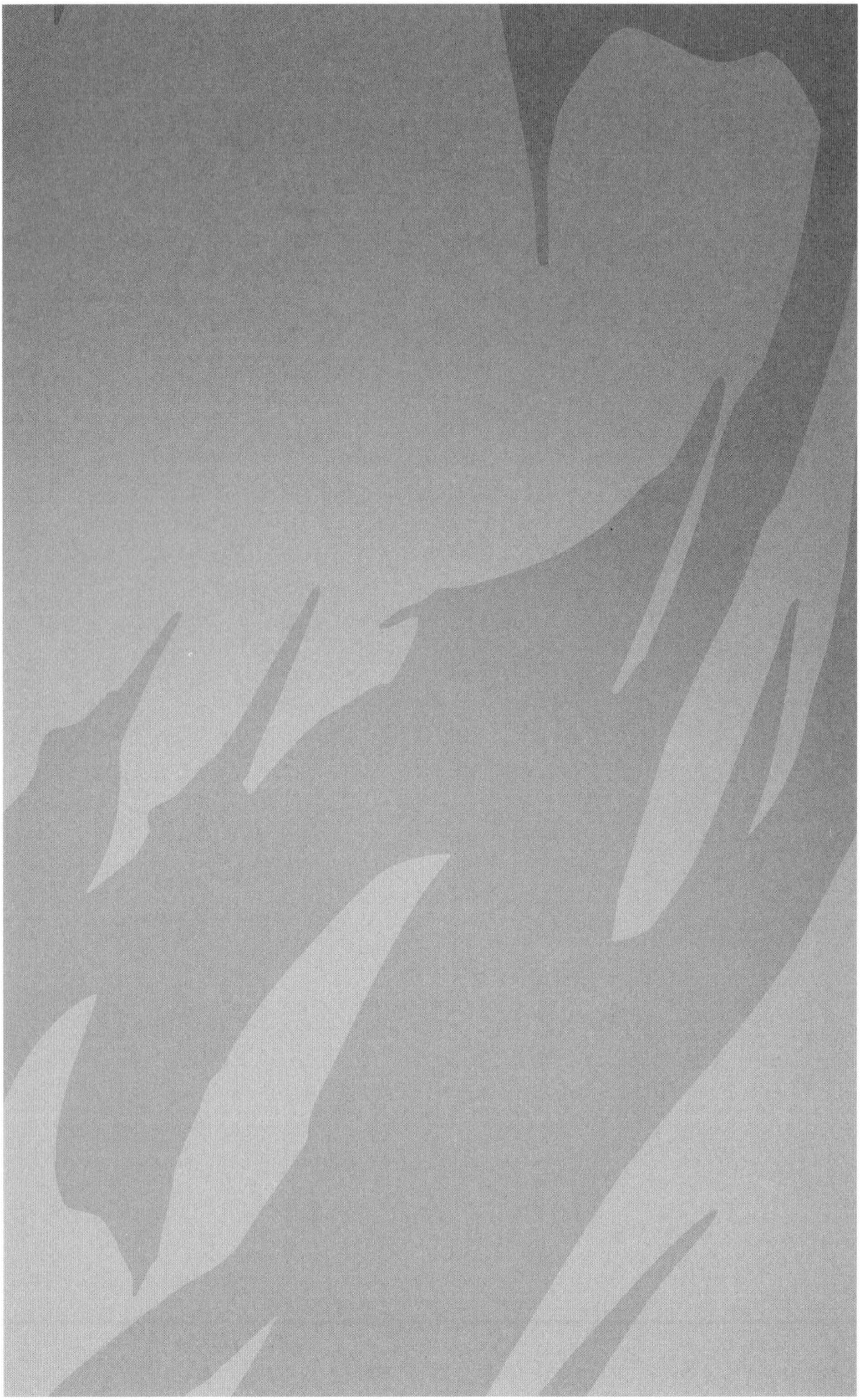

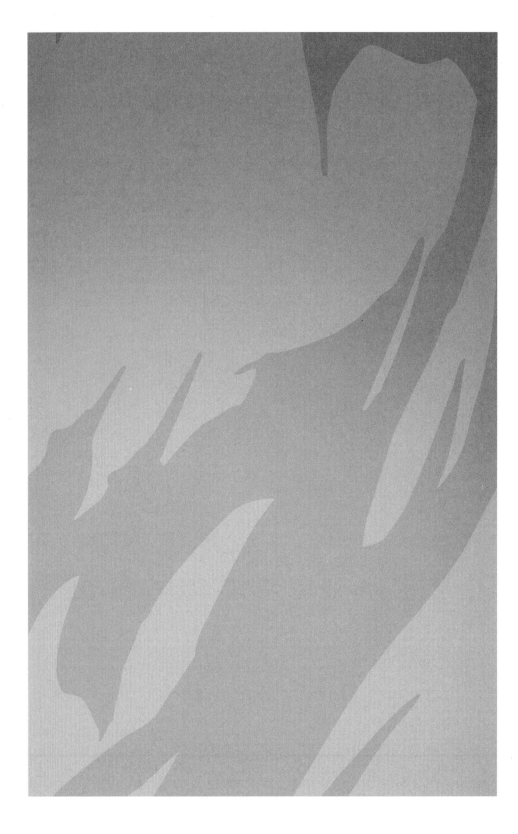

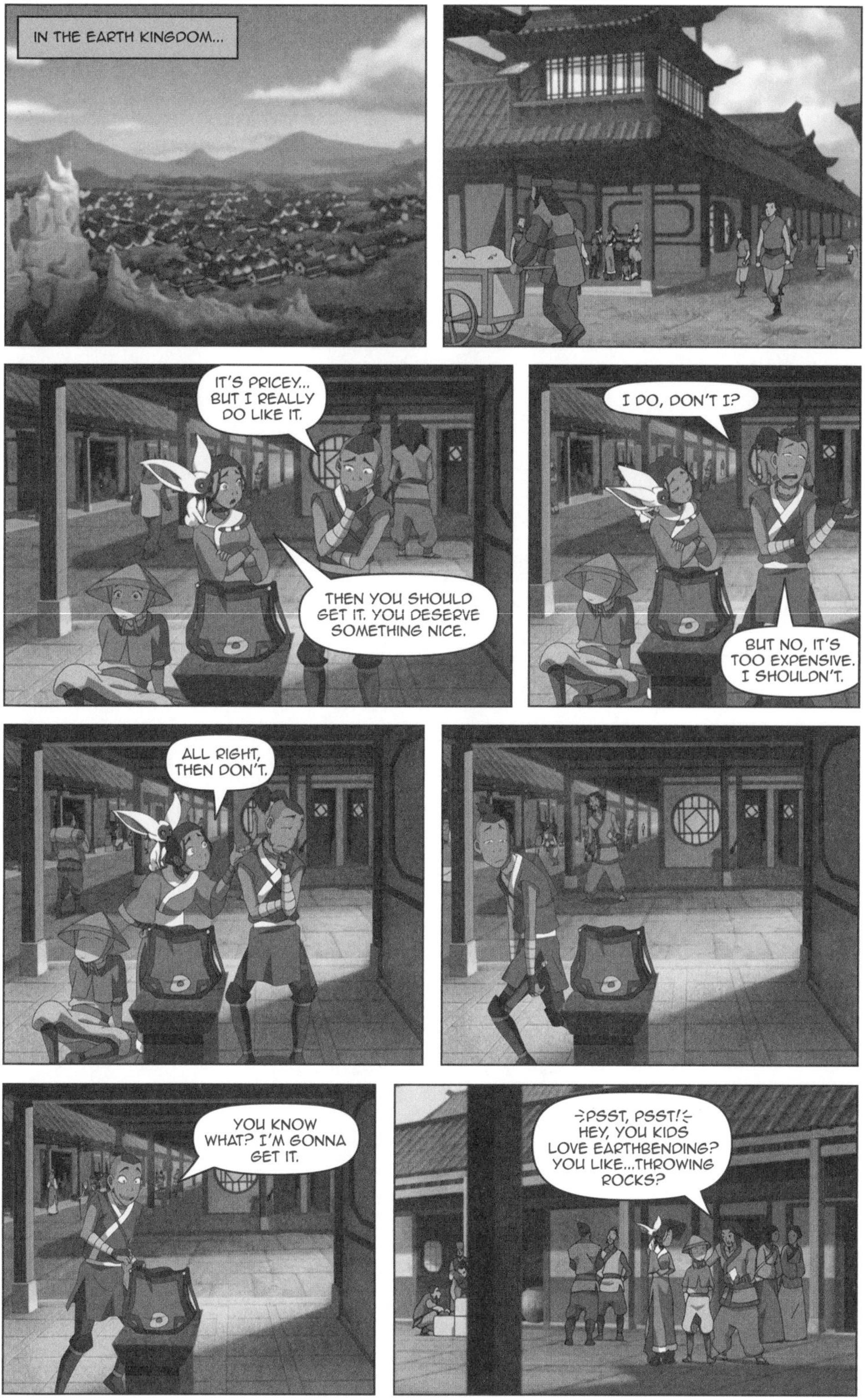
IN THE EARTH KINGDOM...
IT'S PRICEY... BUT I REALLY DO LIKE IT.
THEN YOU SHOULD GET IT. YOU DESERVE SOMETHING NICE.
I DO, DON'T I?
BUT NO, IT'S TOO EXPENSIVE. I SHOULDN'T.
ALL RIGHT, THEN DON'T.
YOU KNOW WHAT? I'M GONNA GET IT.
PSST, PSST! HEY, YOU KIDS LOVE EARTHBENDING? YOU LIKE...THROWING ROCKS?

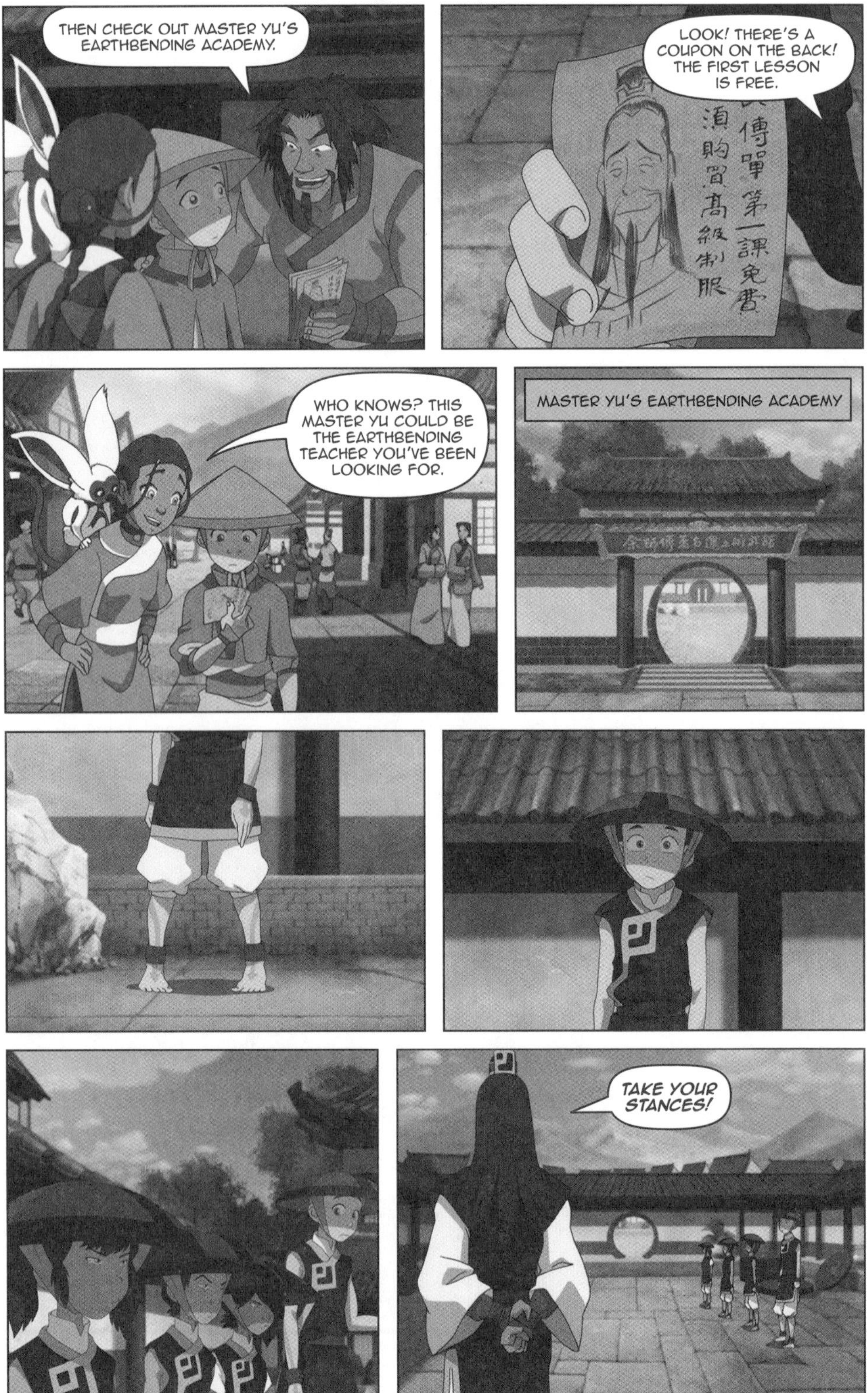
THEN CHECK OUT MASTER YU'S EARTHBENDING ACADEMY.
LOOK! THERE'S A COUPON ON THE BACK! THE FIRST LESSON IS FREE.
傳單第一課免費
須購買高級制服
WHO KNOWS? THIS MASTER YU COULD BE THE EARTHBENDING TEACHER YOU'VE BEEN LOOKING FOR.
MASTER YU'S EARTHBENDING ACADEMY
TAKE YOUR STANCES!

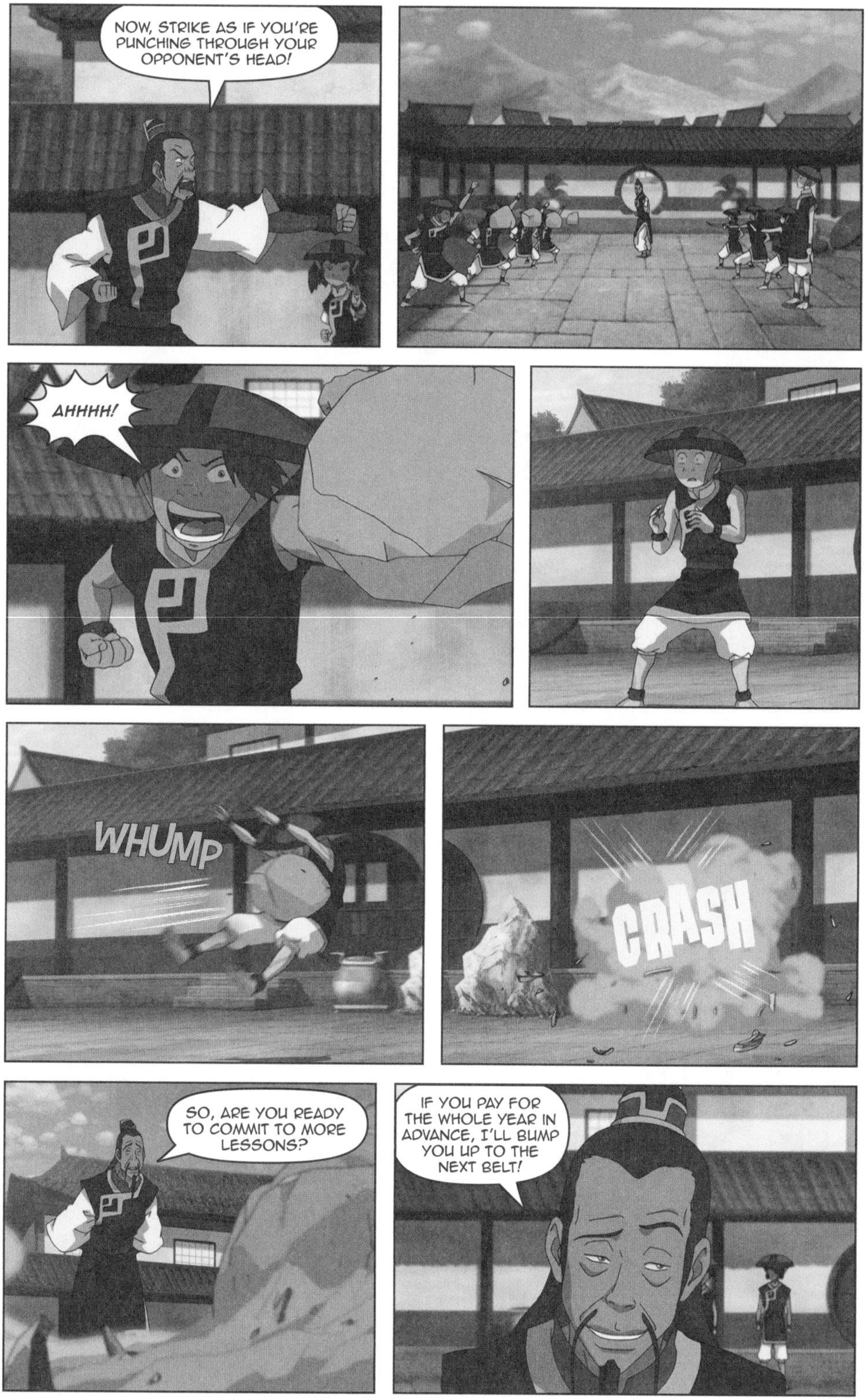
NOW, STRIKE AS IF YOU'RE PUNCHING THROUGH YOUR OPPONENT'S HEAD!
AHHHH!
WHUMP
CRASH
SO, ARE YOU READY TO COMMIT TO MORE LESSONS?
IF YOU PAY FOR THE WHOLE YEAR IN ADVANCE, I'LL BUMP YOU UP TO THE NEXT BELT!

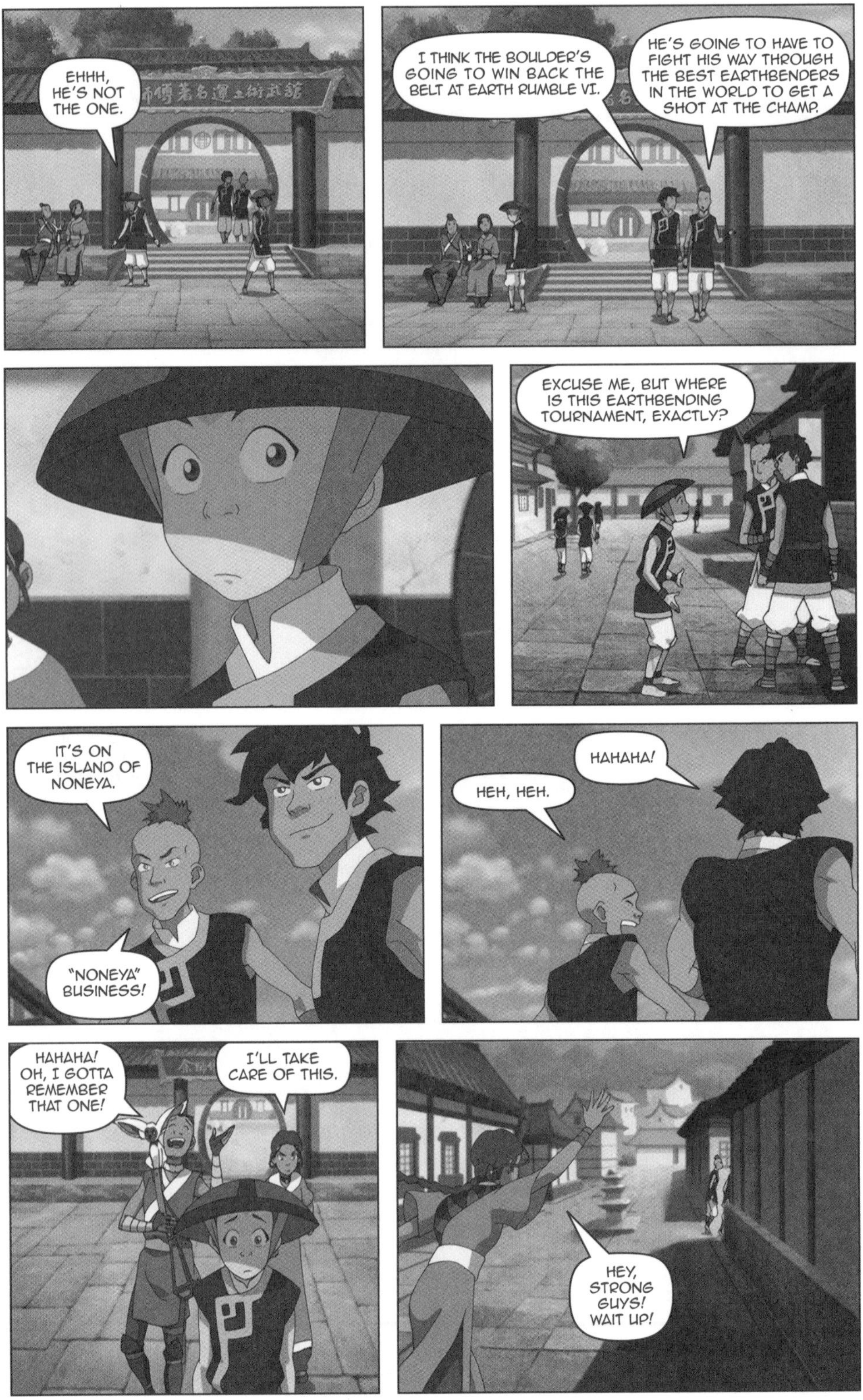
EHHH, HE'S NOT THE ONE.
I THINK THE BOULDER'S GOING TO WIN BACK THE BELT AT EARTH RUMBLE VI.
HE'S GOING TO HAVE TO FIGHT HIS WAY THROUGH THE BEST EARTHBENDERS IN THE WORLD TO GET A SHOT AT THE CHAMP.
EXCUSE ME, BUT WHERE IS THIS EARTHBENDING TOURNAMENT, EXACTLY?
IT'S ON THE ISLAND OF NONEYA.
"NONEYA" BUSINESS!
HAHAHA!
HEH, HEH.
HAHAHA! OH, I GOTTA REMEMBER THAT ONE!
I'LL TAKE CARE OF THIS.
HEY, STRONG GUYS! WAIT UP!

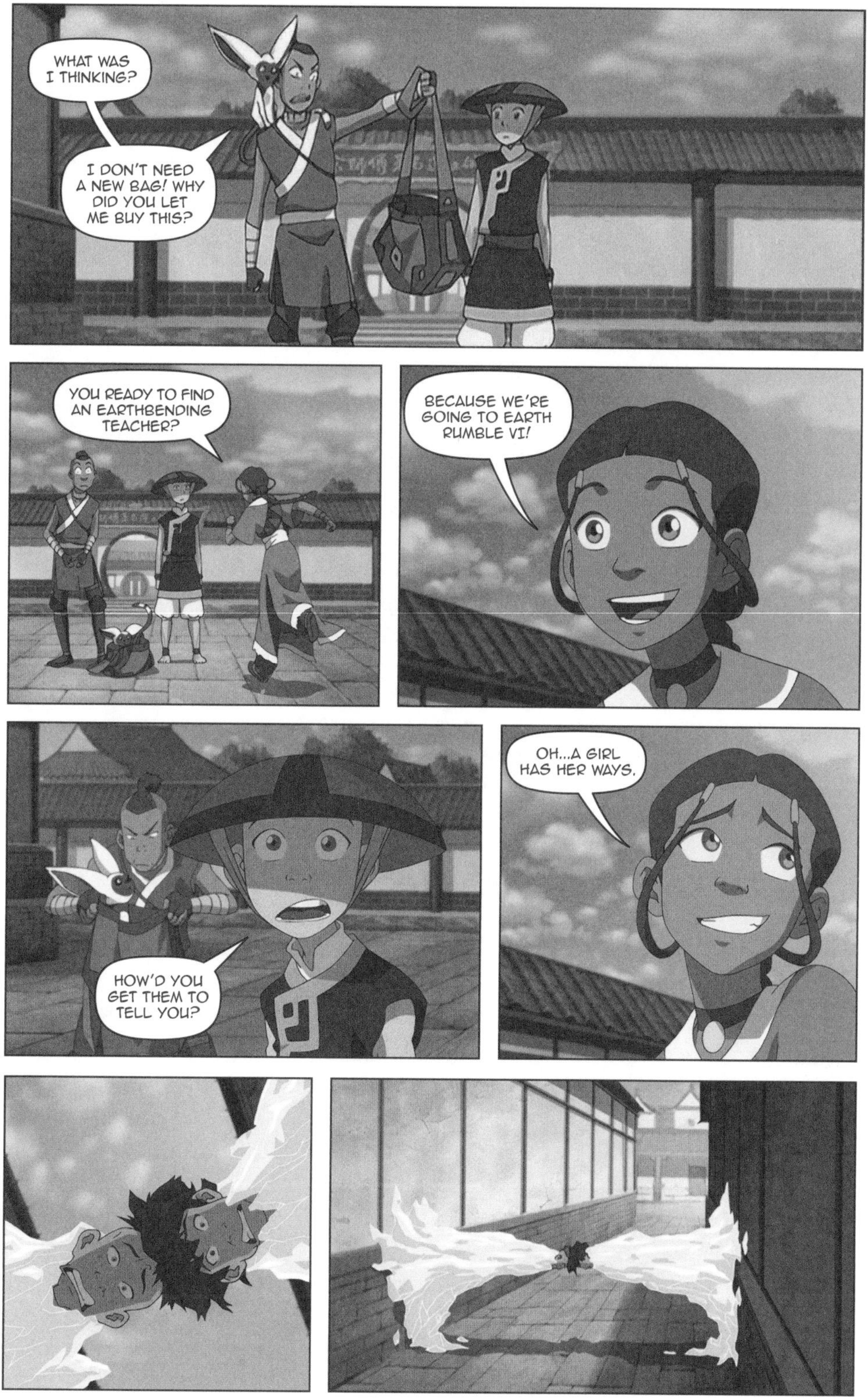
WHAT WAS I THINKING?
I DON'T NEED A NEW BAG! WHY DID YOU LET ME BUY THIS?
YOU READY TO FIND AN EARTHBENDING TEACHER?
BECAUSE WE'RE GOING TO EARTH RUMBLE VI!
HOW'D YOU GET THEM TO TELL YOU?
OH...A GIRL HAS HER WAYS.

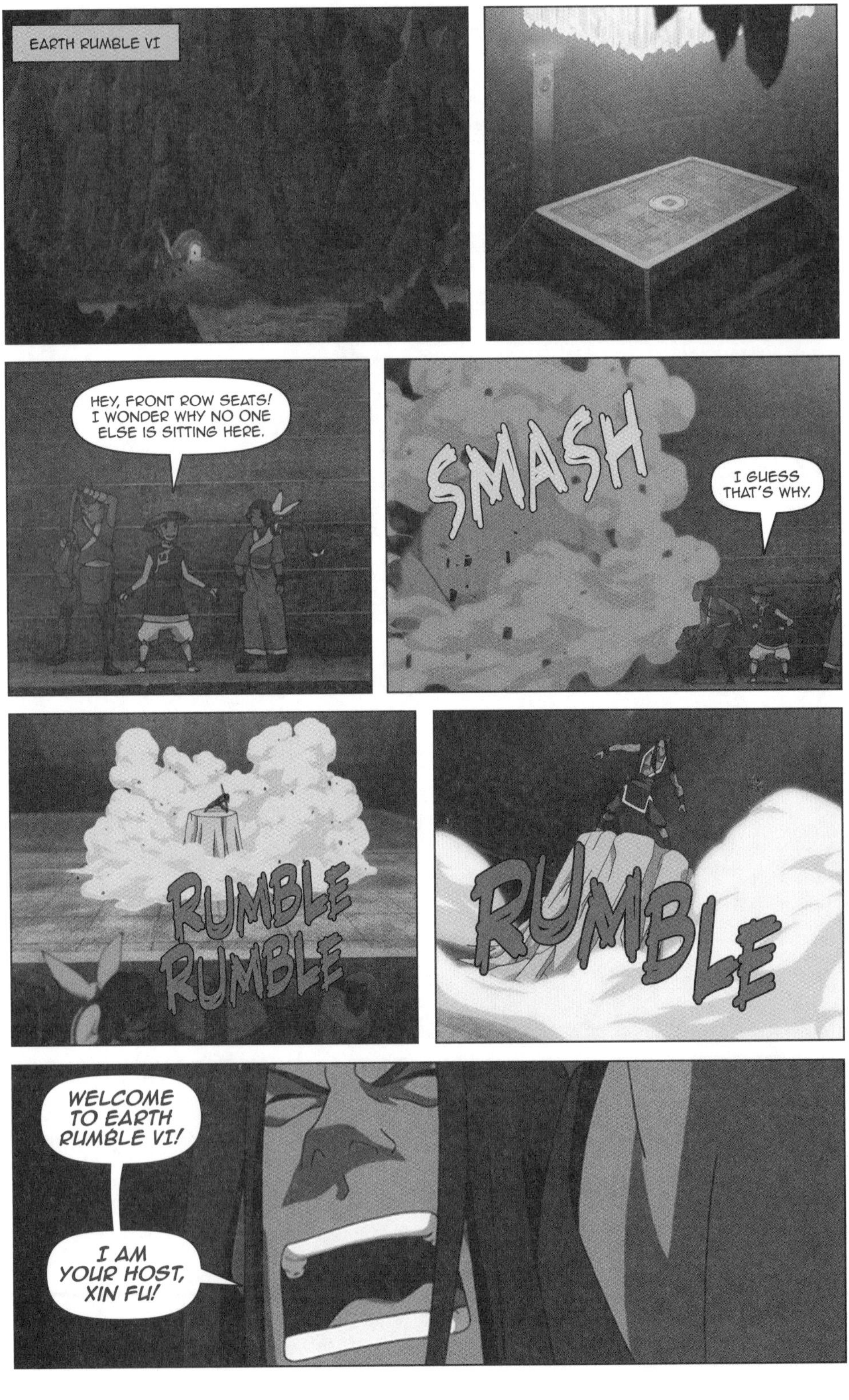
EARTH RUMBLE VI
HEY, FRONT ROW SEATS! I WONDER WHY NO ONE ELSE IS SITTING HERE.
SMASH
I GUESS THAT'S WHY.
RUMBLE RUMBLE
RUMBLE
WELCOME TO EARTH RUMBLE VI!
I AM YOUR HOST, XIN FU!

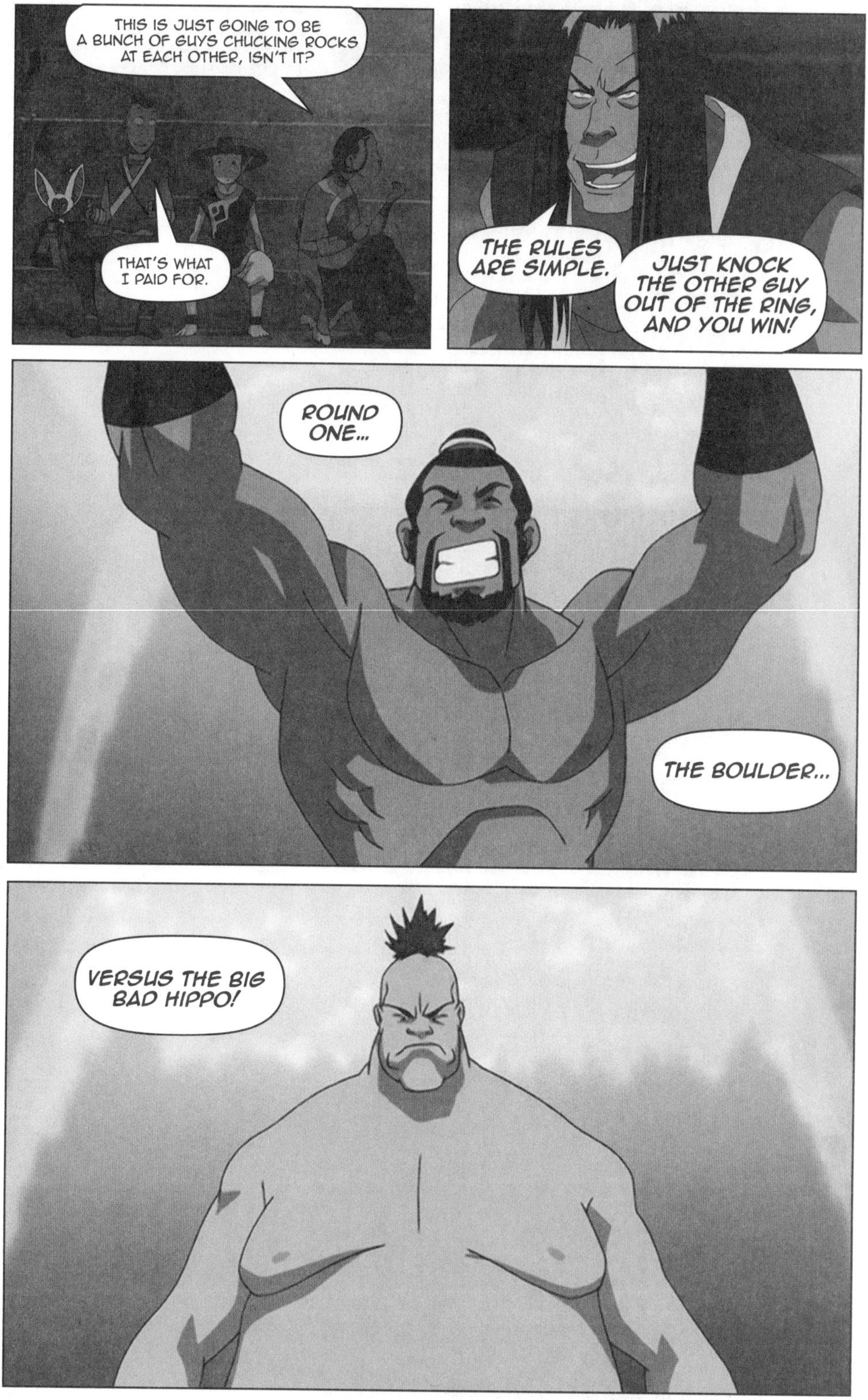
THIS IS JUST GOING TO BE A BUNCH OF GUYS CHUCKING ROCKS AT EACH OTHER, ISN'T IT?
THAT'S WHAT I PAID FOR.
THE RULES ARE SIMPLE.
JUST KNOCK THE OTHER GUY OUT OF THE RING, AND YOU WIN!
ROUND ONE...
THE BOULDER...
VERSUS THE BIG BAD HIPPO!

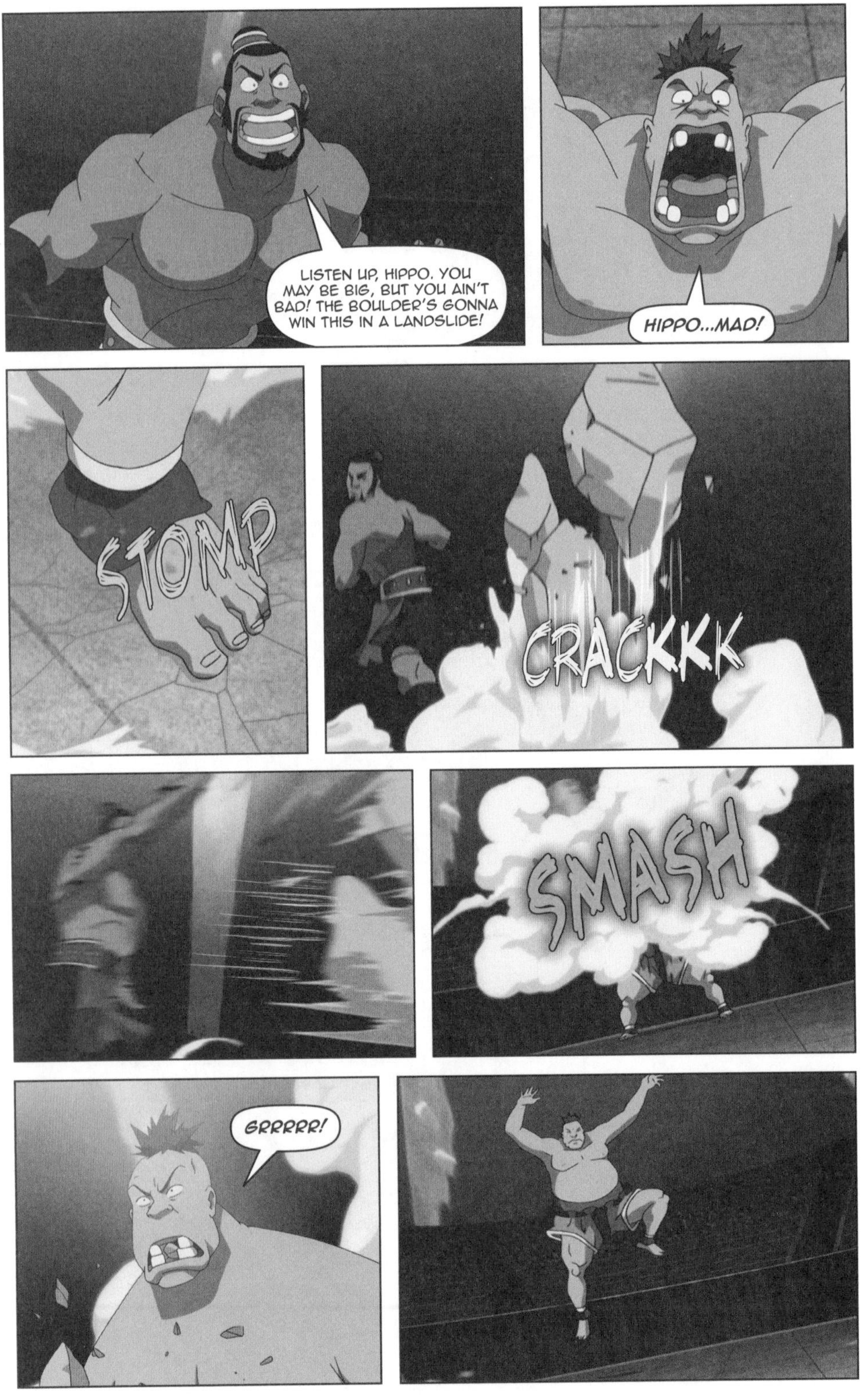
LISTEN UP, HIPPO. YOU MAY BE BIG, BUT YOU AIN'T BAD! THE BOULDER'S GONNA WIN THIS IN A LANDSLIDE!
HIPPO...MAD!
STOMP
CRACKKK
SMASH
GRRRRR!

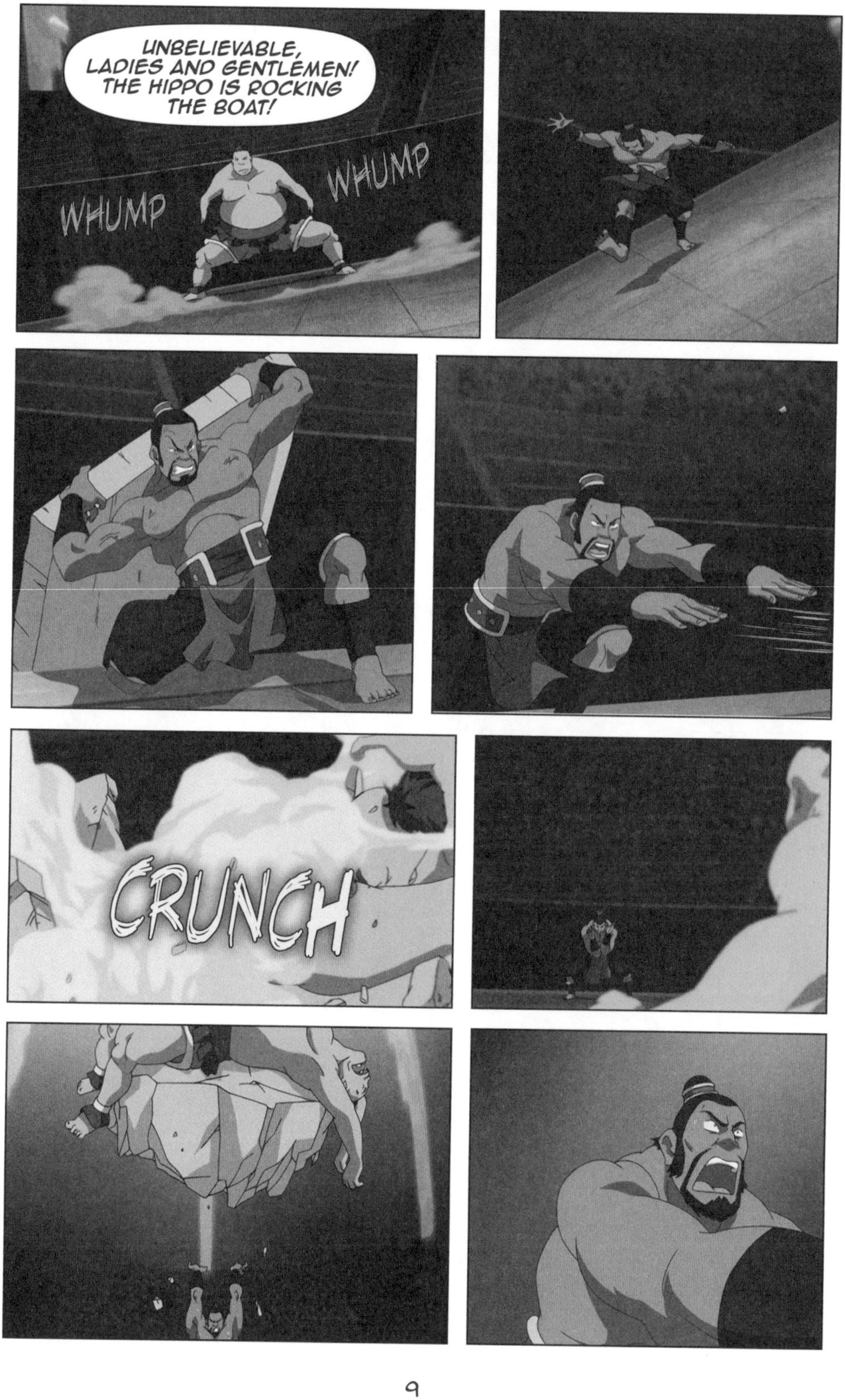
UNBELIEVABLE, LADIES AND GENTLEMEN! THE HIPPO IS ROCKING THE BOAT!
WHUMP
WHUMP
CRUNCH

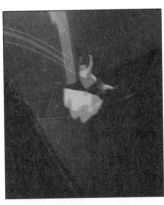

THE BOULDER WINS!

HOW ABOUT THE BOULDER? HE'S GOT SOME GOOD MOVES.

I DON'T KNOW. BUMI SAID I NEED A TEACHER WHO LISTENS TO THE EARTH. HE'S JUST LISTENING TO HIS BIG MUSCLES. WHAT DO YOU THINK, SOKKA?

WHOO-HOO!

EARTH RUMBLE VI CONTINUES WITH MORE ACTION-PACKED BATTLES...

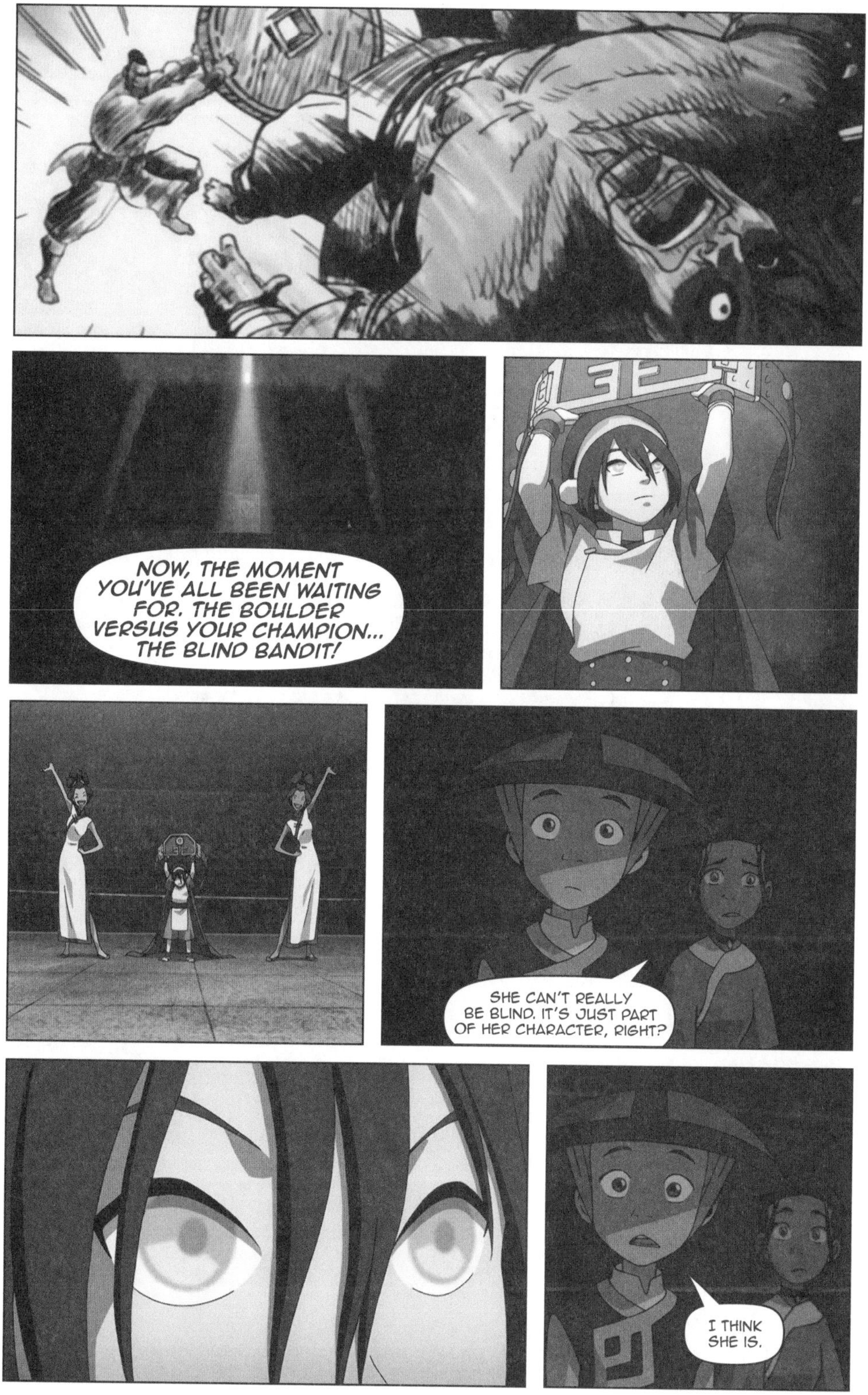
NOW, THE MOMENT YOU'VE ALL BEEN WAITING FOR. THE BOULDER VERSUS YOUR CHAMPION... THE BLIND BANDIT!
SHE CAN'T REALLY BE BLIND. IT'S JUST PART OF HER CHARACTER, RIGHT?
I THINK SHE IS.

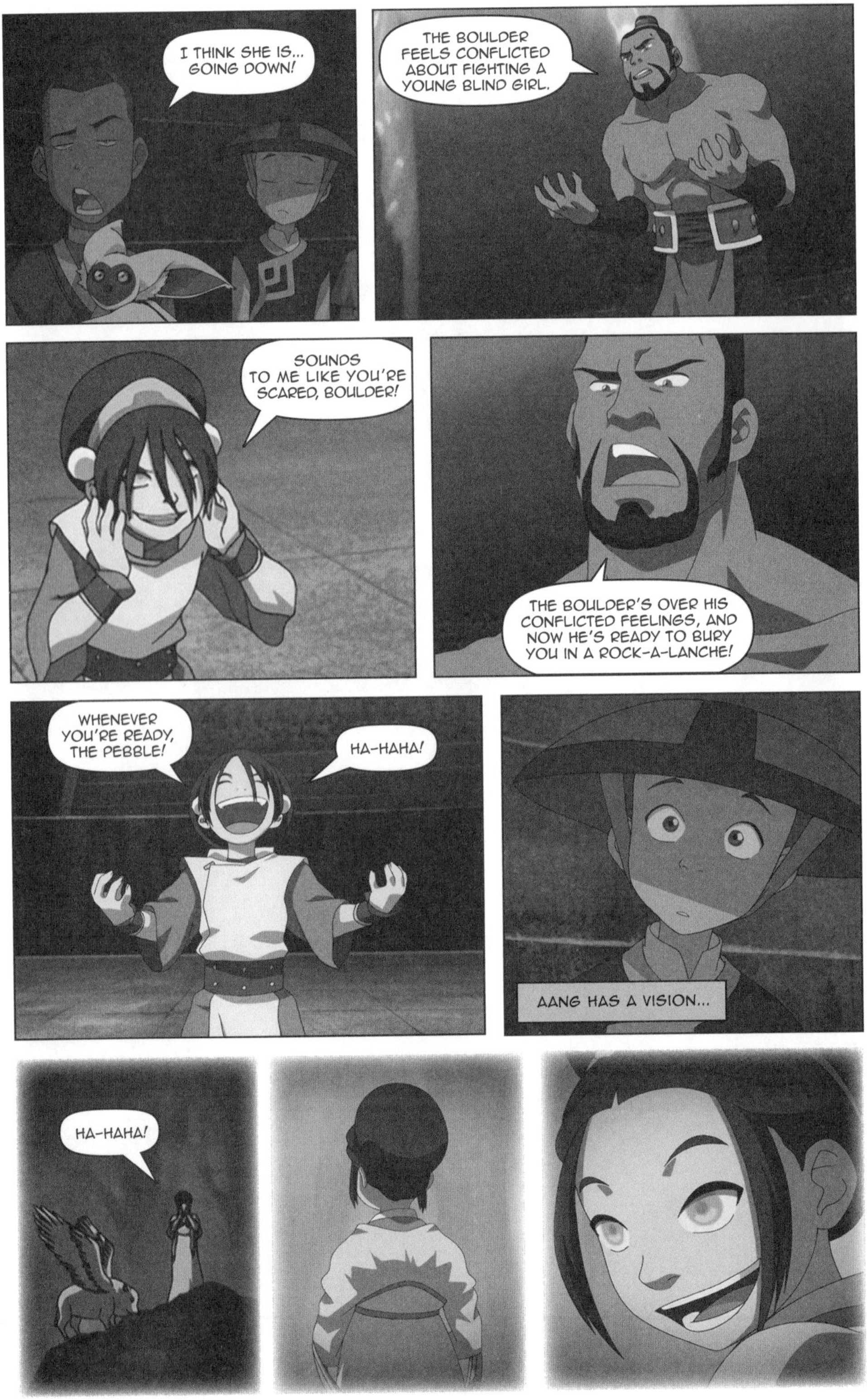
I THINK SHE IS... GOING DOWN!
THE BOULDER FEELS CONFLICTED ABOUT FIGHTING A YOUNG BLIND GIRL.
SOUNDS TO ME LIKE YOU'RE SCARED, BOULDER!
THE BOULDER'S OVER HIS CONFLICTED FEELINGS, AND NOW HE'S READY TO BURY YOU IN A ROCK-A-LANCHE!
WHENEVER YOU'RE READY, THE PEBBLE!
HA-HAHA!
AANG HAS A VISION...
HA-HAHA!

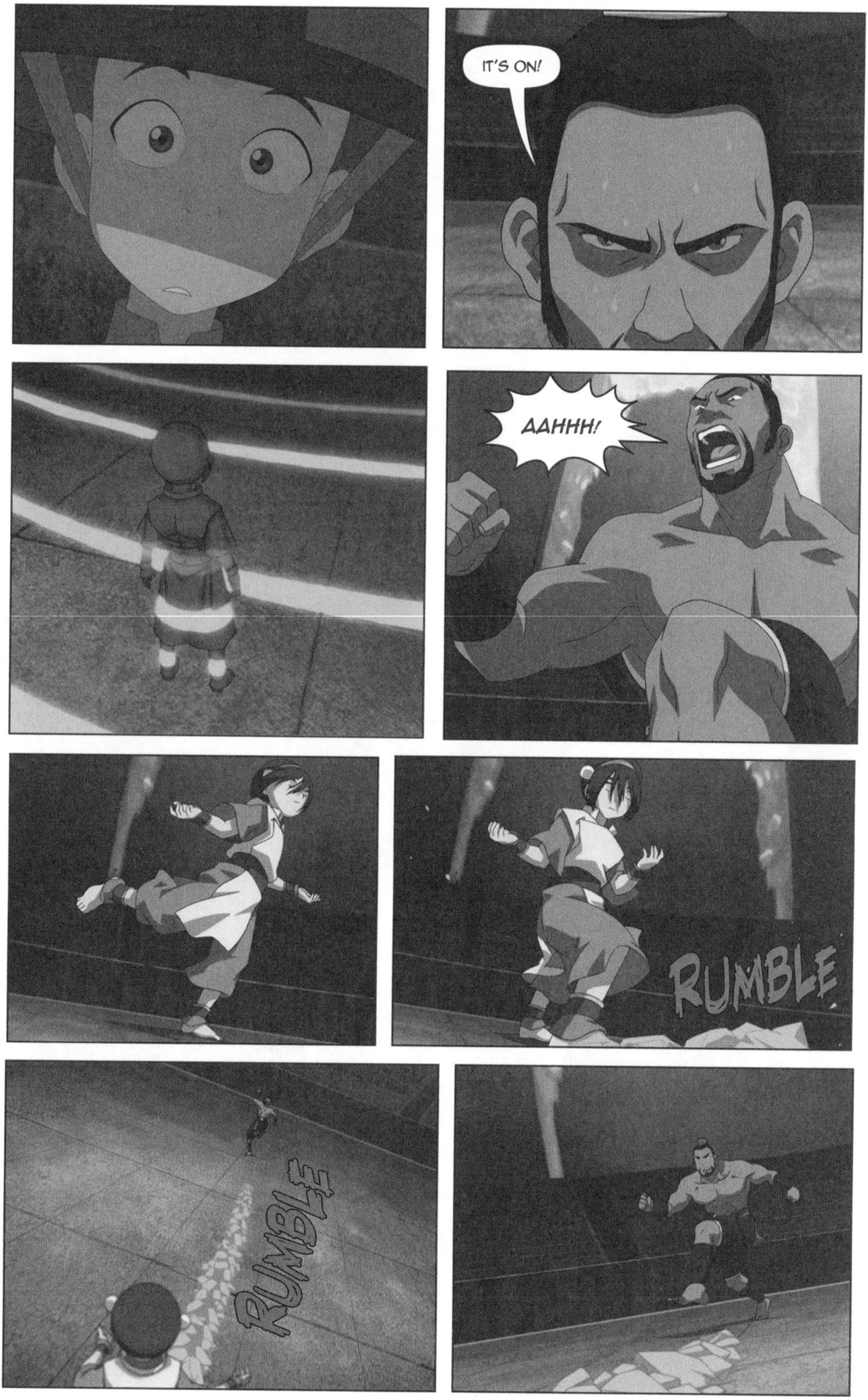
IT'S ON!
AAHHH!
RUMBLE
RUMBLE

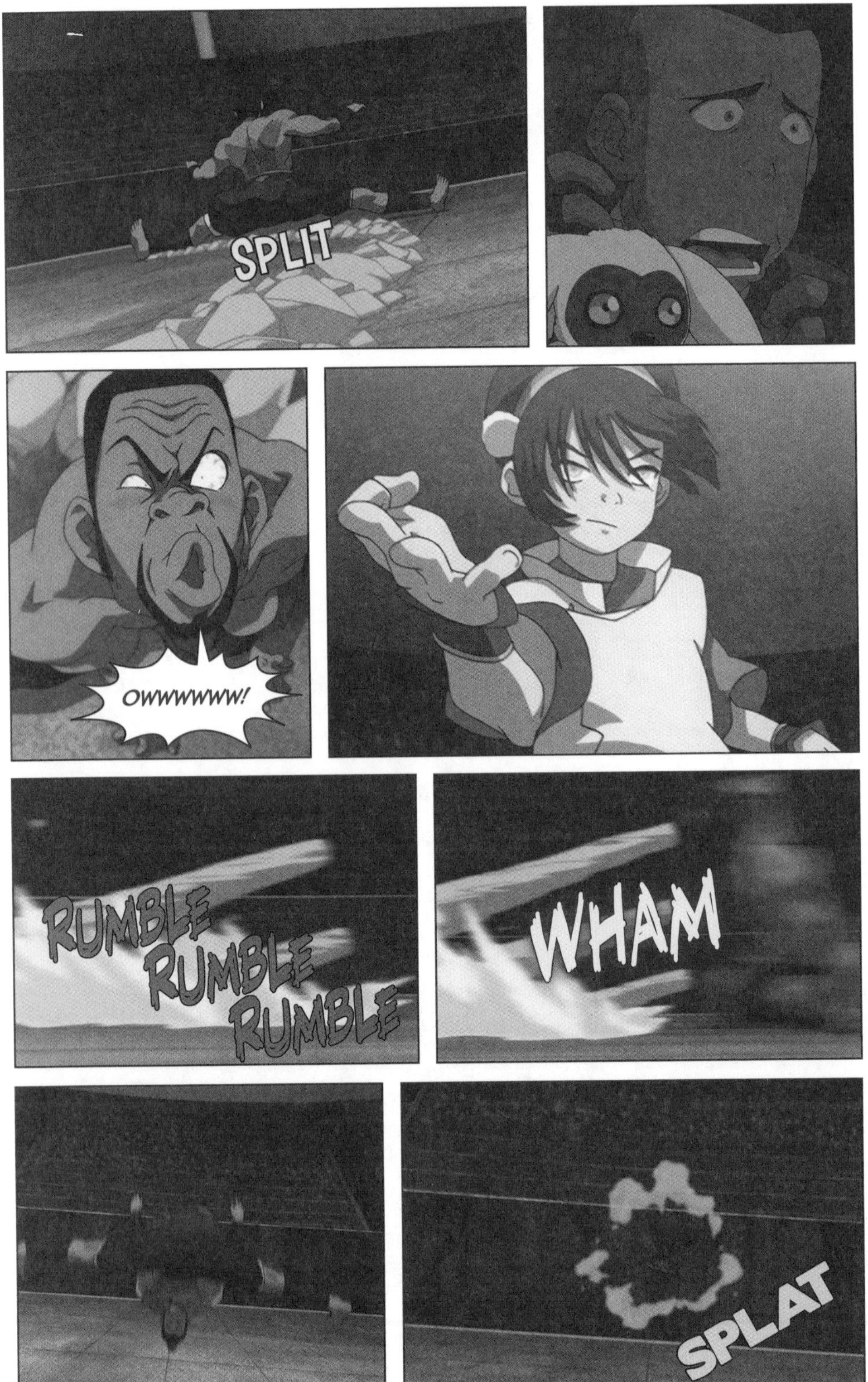
SPLIT
OWWWWWW!
RUMBLE
RUMBLE
RUMBLE
WHAM
SPLAT

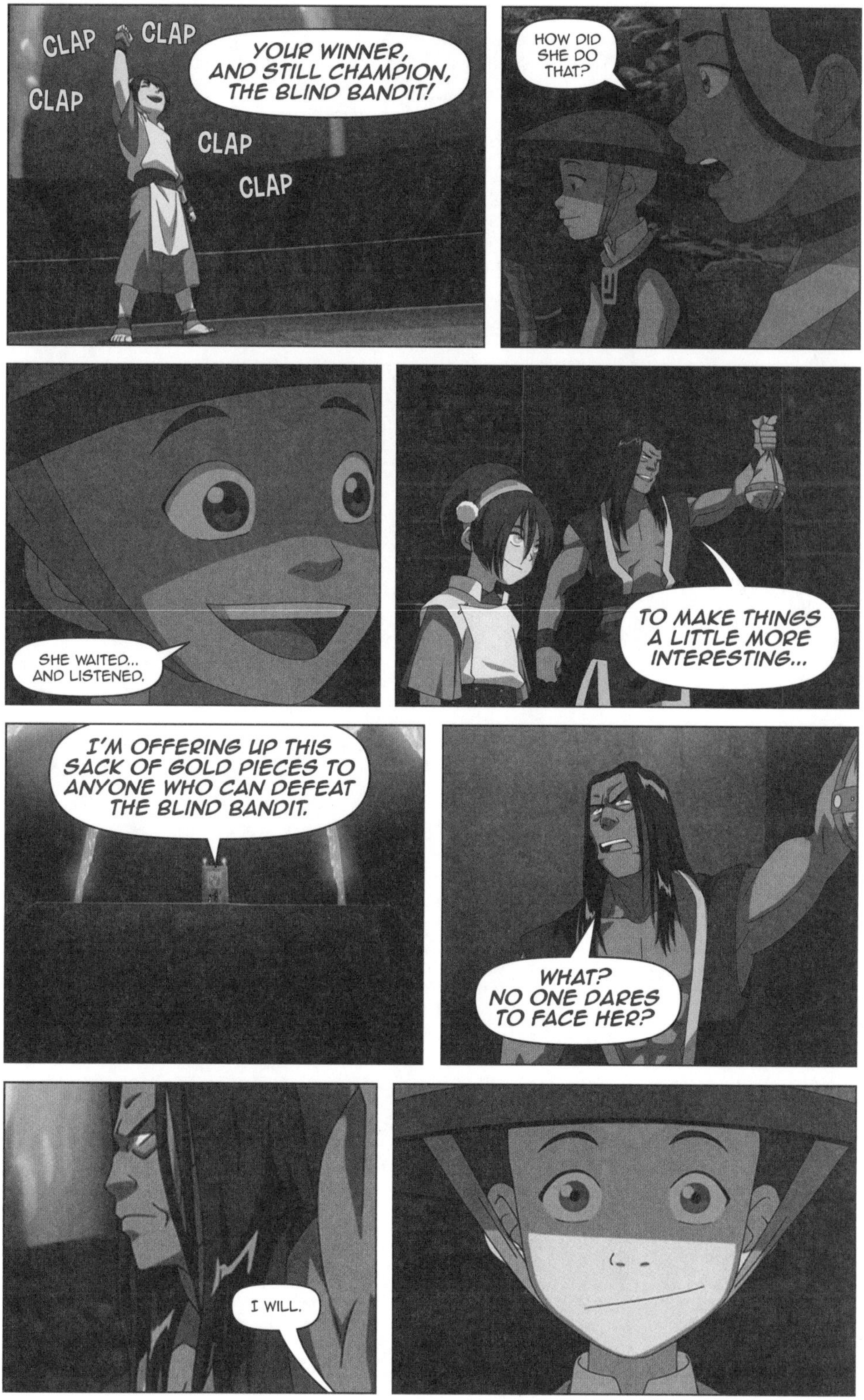
CLAP CLAP
CLAP
CLAP
CLAP
YOUR WINNER, AND STILL CHAMPION, THE BLIND BANDIT!
HOW DID SHE DO THAT?
SHE WAITED... AND LISTENED.
TO MAKE THINGS A LITTLE MORE INTERESTING...
I'M OFFERING UP THIS SACK OF GOLD PIECES TO ANYONE WHO CAN DEFEAT THE BLIND BANDIT.
WHAT? NO ONE DARES TO FACE HER?
I WILL.

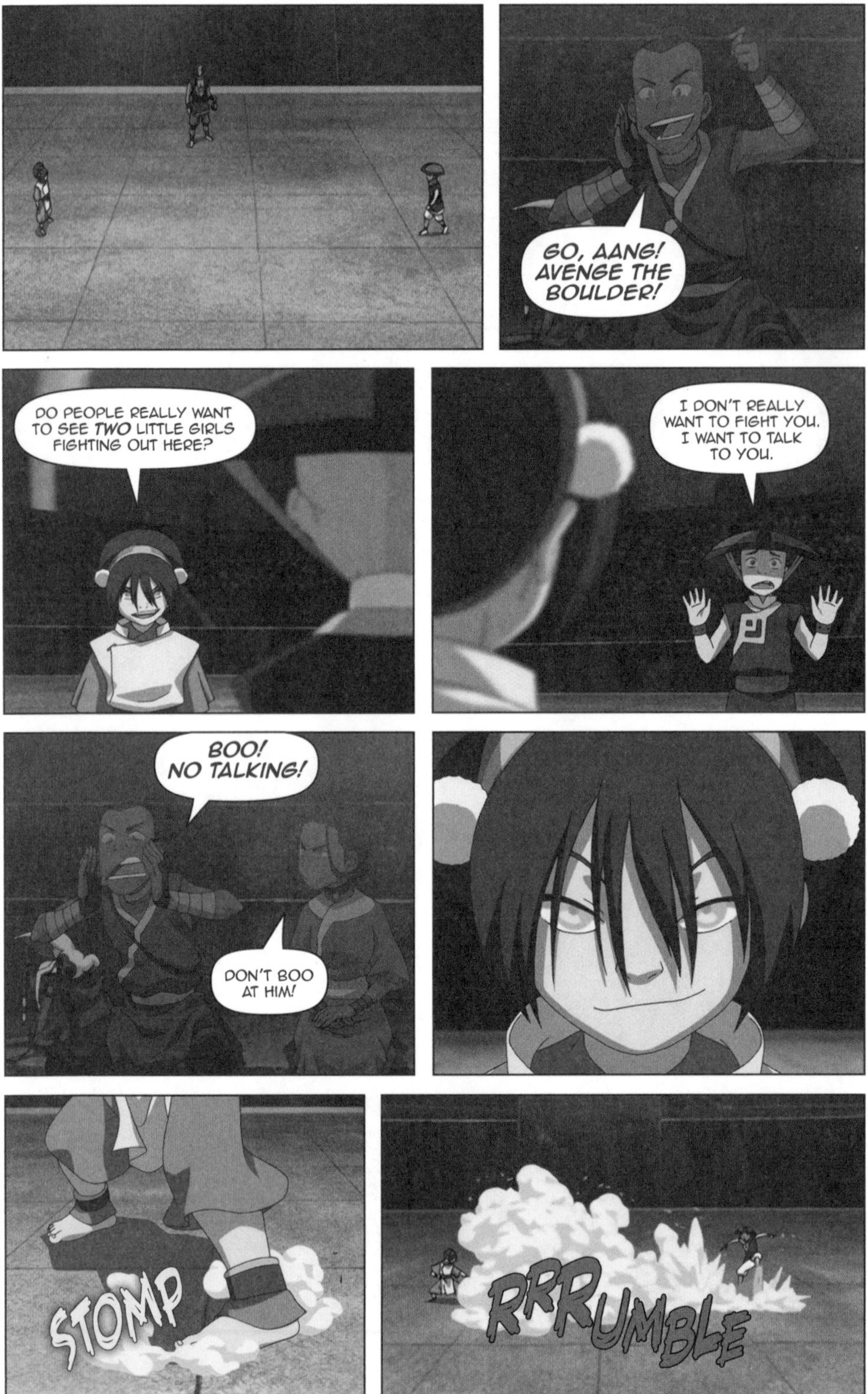
GO, AANG! AVENGE THE BOULDER!
DO PEOPLE REALLY WANT TO SEE TWO LITTLE GIRLS FIGHTING OUT HERE?
I DON'T REALLY WANT TO FIGHT YOU. I WANT TO TALK TO YOU.
BOO! NO TALKING!
DON'T BOO AT HIM!
STOMP
RRRUMBLE

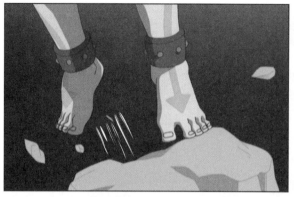

SOMEBODY'S A LITTLE LIGHT ON HIS FEET! WHAT'S YOUR FIGHTING NAME?

THE FANCY DANCER?

RUMBLE RUMBLE

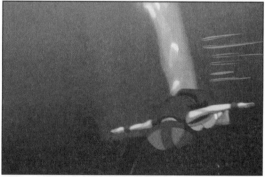

WHERE'D YOU GO?

PLEASE, WAIT!

THERE YOU ARE!

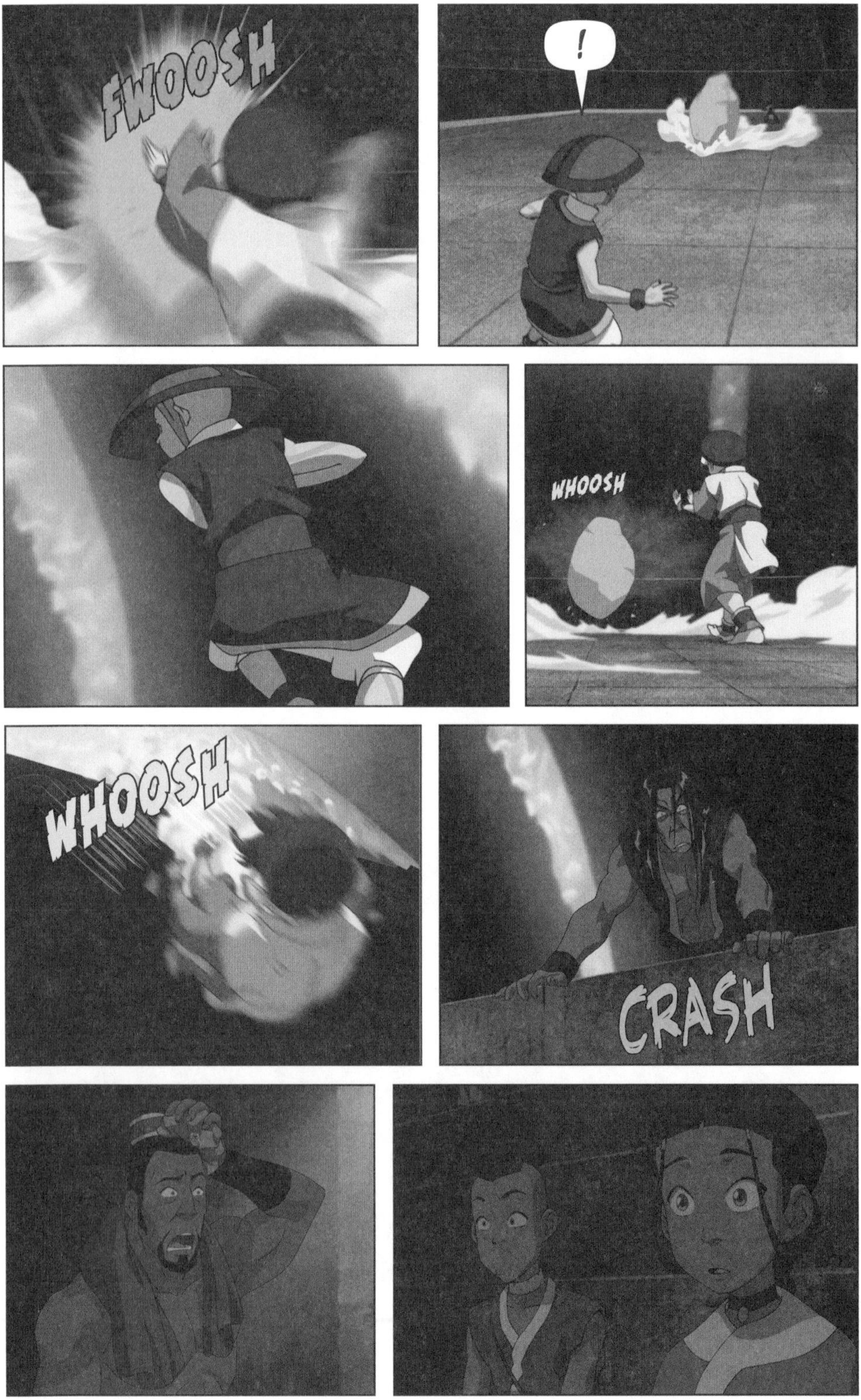
FWOOSH
!
WHOOSH
WHOOSH
CRASH

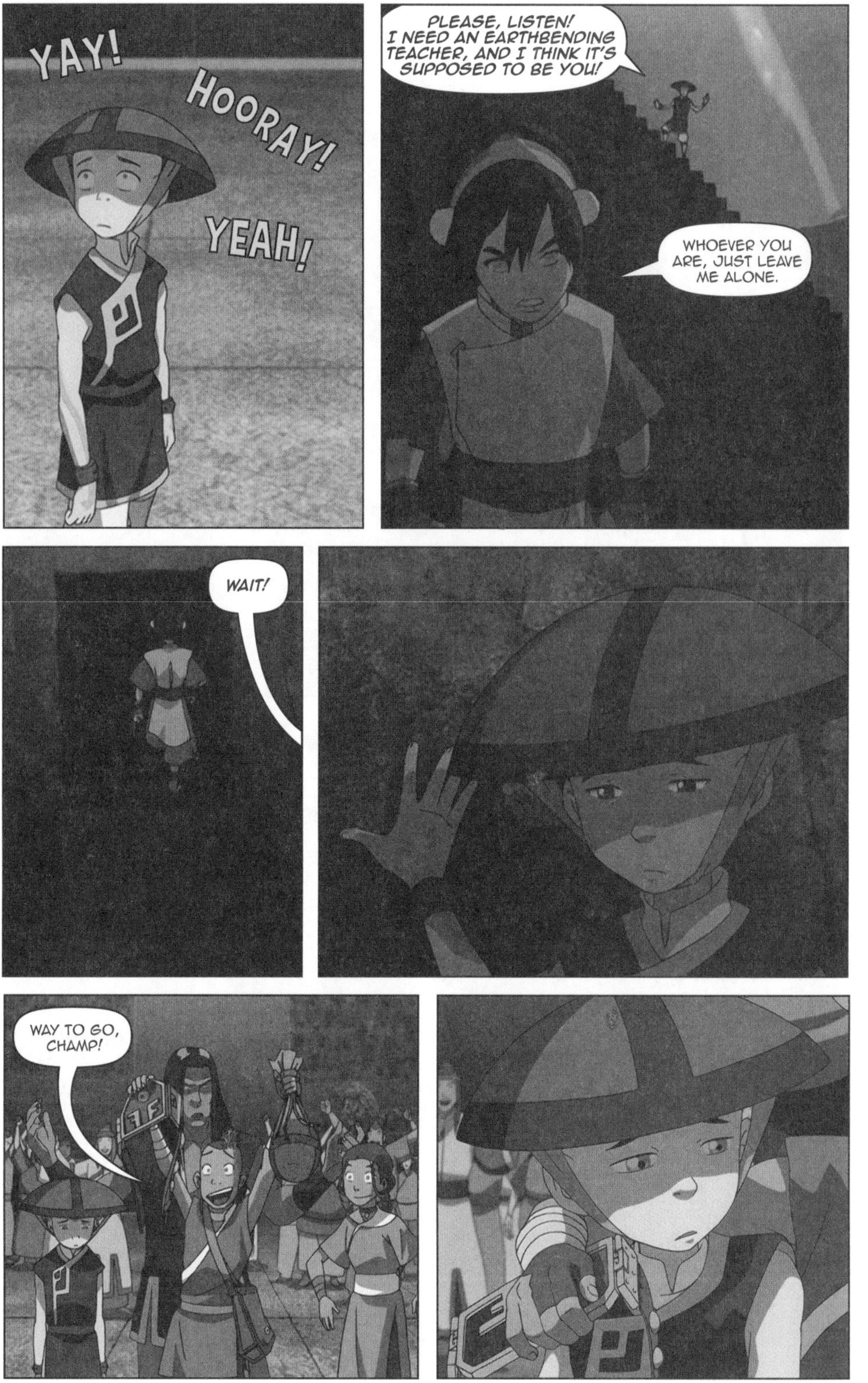
YAY!
HOORAY!
YEAH!
PLEASE, LISTEN! I NEED AN EARTHBENDING TEACHER, AND I THINK IT'S SUPPOSED TO BE YOU!
WHOEVER YOU ARE, JUST LEAVE ME ALONE.
WAIT!
WAY TO GO, CHAMP!

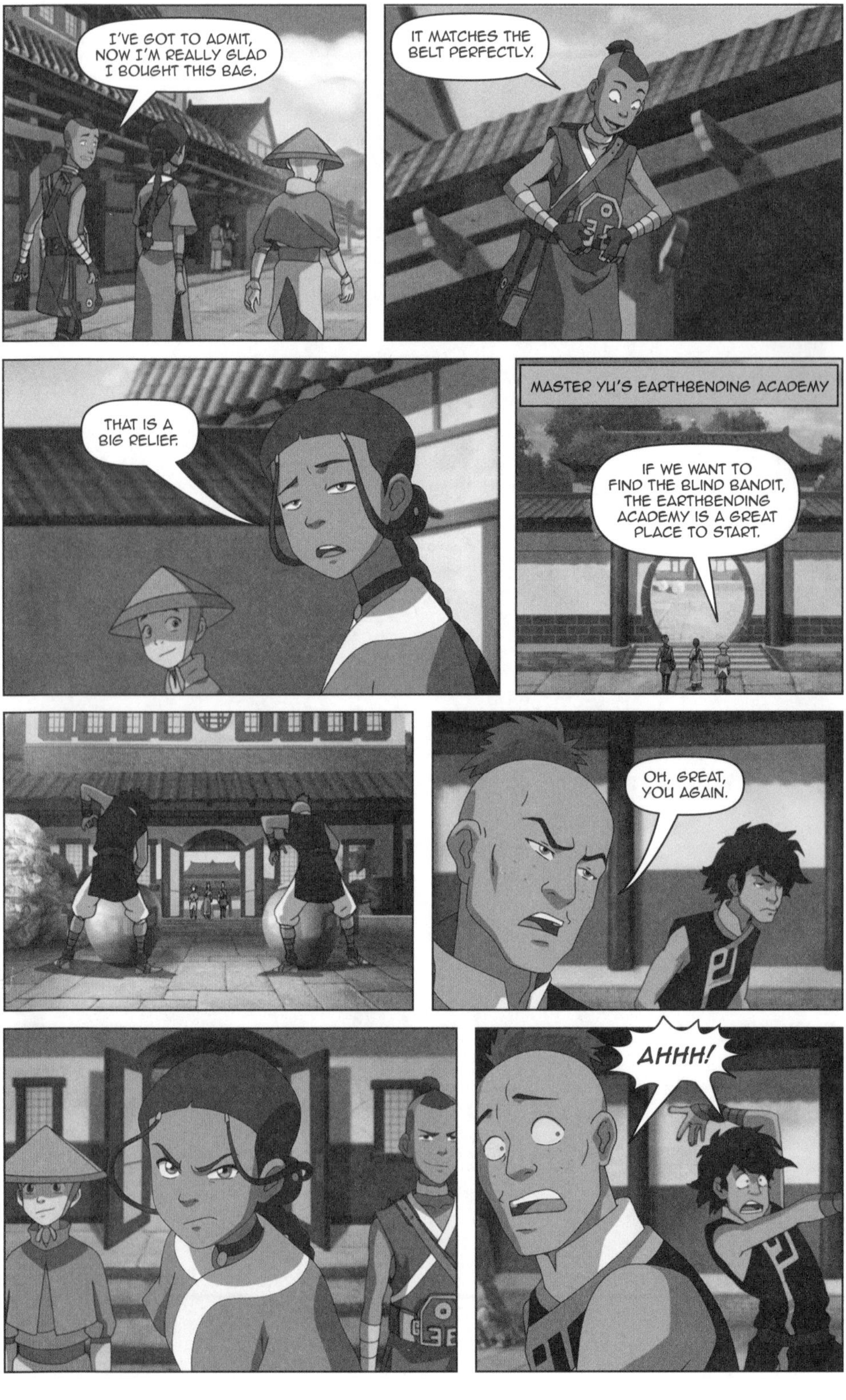
I'VE GOT TO ADMIT, NOW I'M REALLY GLAD I BOUGHT THIS BAG.
IT MATCHES THE BELT PERFECTLY.
THAT IS A BIG RELIEF.
MASTER YU'S EARTHBENDING ACADEMY
IF WE WANT TO FIND THE BLIND BANDIT, THE EARTHBENDING ACADEMY IS A GREAT PLACE TO START.
OH, GREAT, YOU AGAIN.
AHHH!

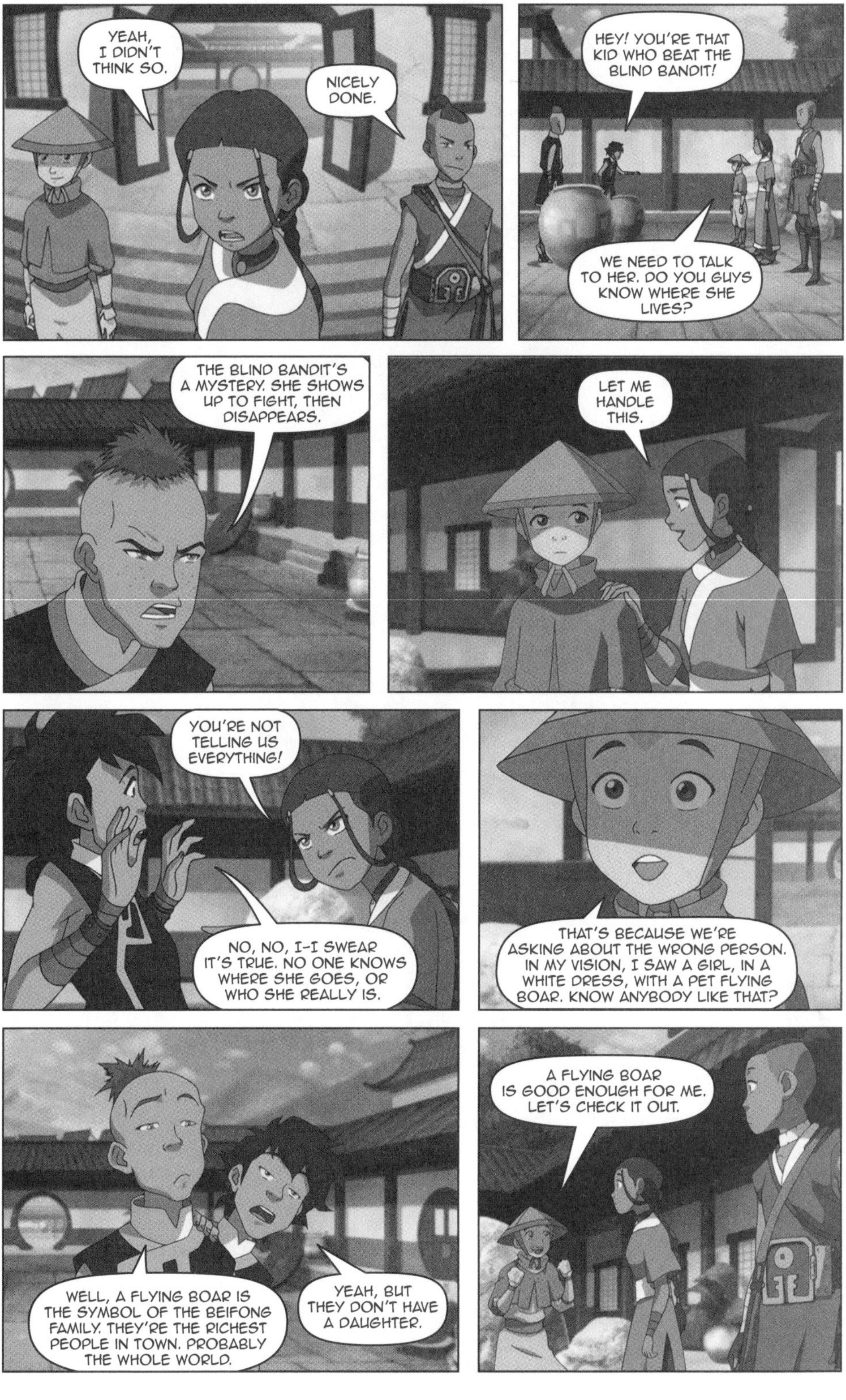
YEAH, I DIDN'T THINK SO.
NICELY DONE.
HEY! YOU'RE THAT KID WHO BEAT THE BLIND BANDIT!
WE NEED TO TALK TO HER. DO YOU GUYS KNOW WHERE SHE LIVES?
THE BLIND BANDIT'S A MYSTERY. SHE SHOWS UP TO FIGHT, THEN DISAPPEARS.
LET ME HANDLE THIS.
YOU'RE NOT TELLING US EVERYTHING!
NO, NO, I-I SWEAR IT'S TRUE. NO ONE KNOWS WHERE SHE GOES, OR WHO SHE REALLY IS.
THAT'S BECAUSE WE'RE ASKING ABOUT THE WRONG PERSON. IN MY VISION, I SAW A GIRL, IN A WHITE DRESS, WITH A PET FLYING BOAR. KNOW ANYBODY LIKE THAT?
WELL, A FLYING BOAR IS THE SYMBOL OF THE BEIFONG FAMILY. THEY'RE THE RICHEST PEOPLE IN TOWN. PROBABLY THE WHOLE WORLD.
YEAH, BUT THEY DON'T HAVE A DAUGHTER.
A FLYING BOAR IS GOOD ENOUGH FOR ME. LET'S CHECK IT OUT.

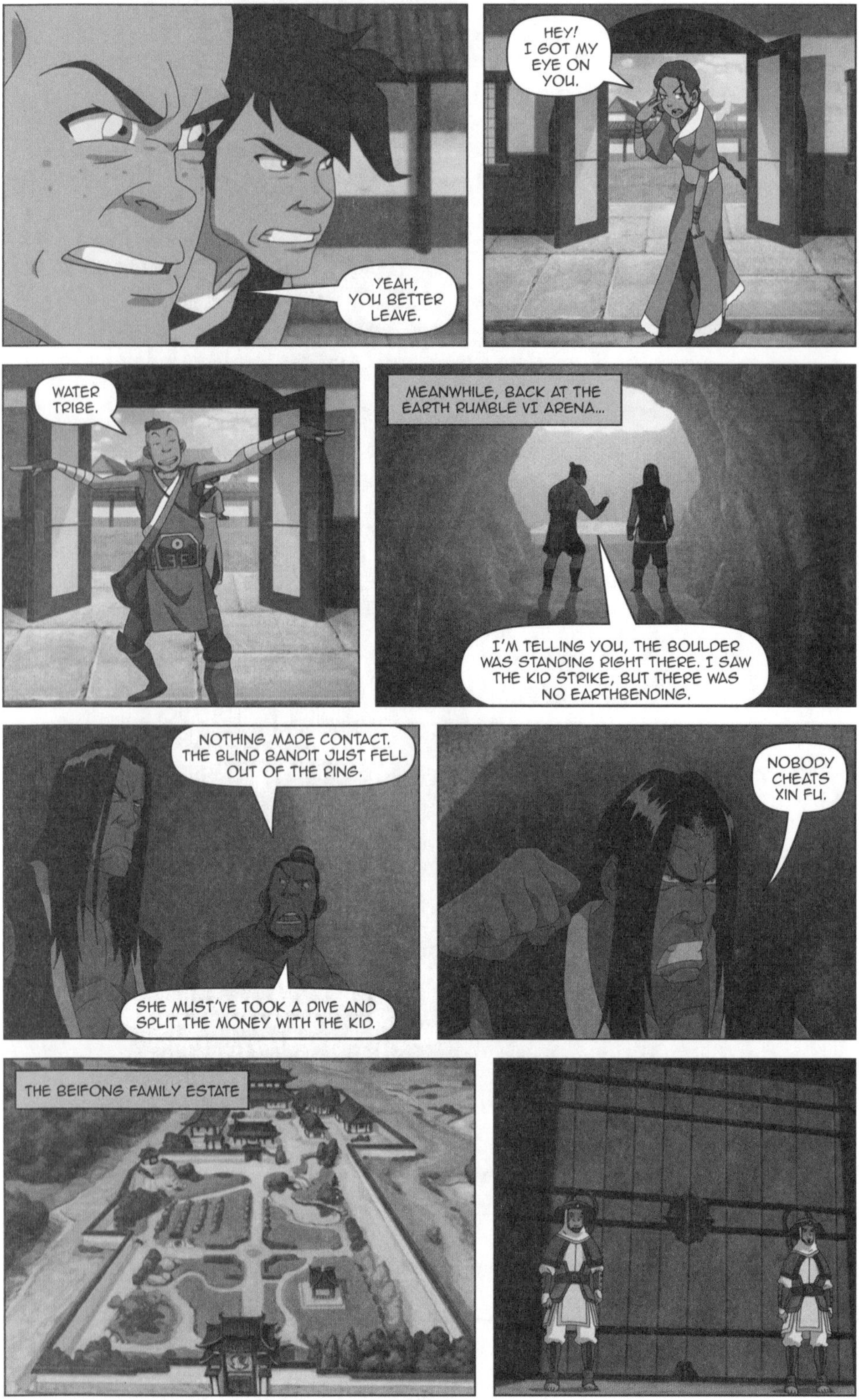
YEAH, YOU BETTER LEAVE.
HEY! I GOT MY EYE ON YOU.
WATER TRIBE.
MEANWHILE, BACK AT THE EARTH RUMBLE VI ARENA...
I'M TELLING YOU, THE BOULDER WAS STANDING RIGHT THERE. I SAW THE KID STRIKE, BUT THERE WAS NO EARTHBENDING.
NOTHING MADE CONTACT. THE BLIND BANDIT JUST FELL OUT OF THE RING.
SHE MUST'VE TOOK A DIVE AND SPLIT THE MONEY WITH THE KID.
NOBODY CHEATS XIN FU.
THE BEIFONG FAMILY ESTATE

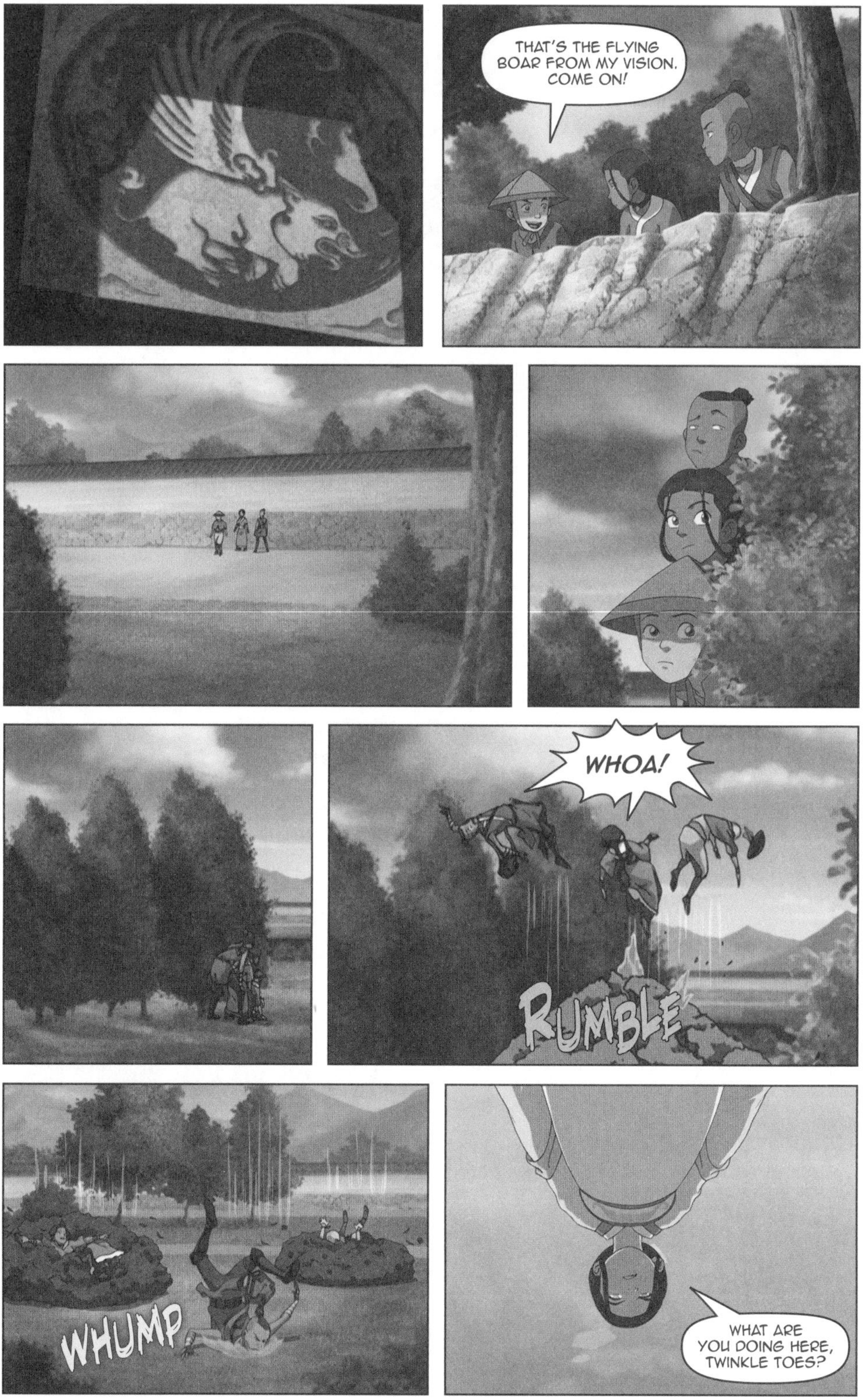
THAT'S THE FLYING BOAR FROM MY VISION. COME ON!
WHOA!
RUMBLE
WHUMP
WHAT ARE YOU DOING HERE, TWINKLE TOES?

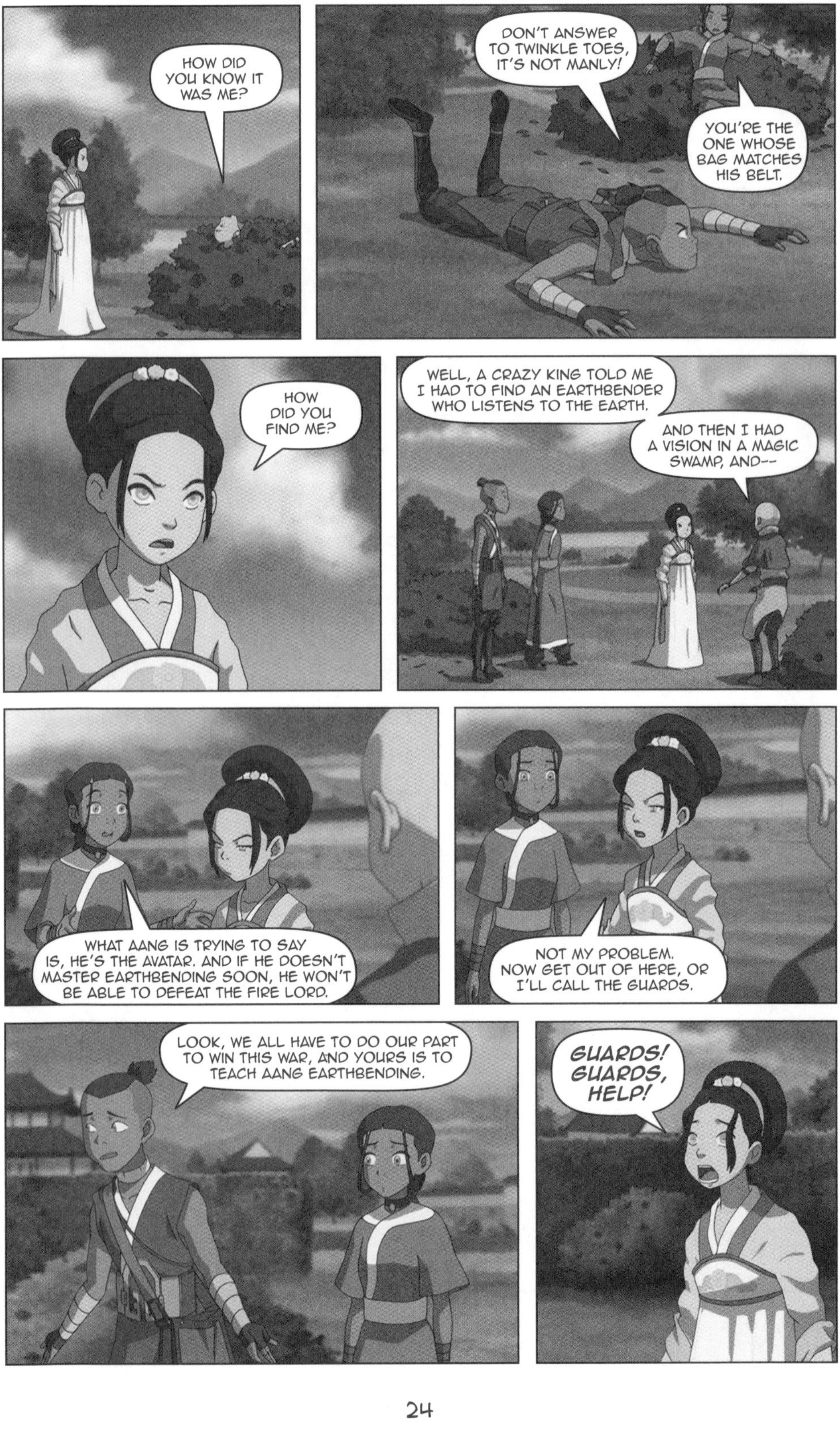
HOW DID YOU KNOW IT WAS ME?
DON'T ANSWER TO TWINKLE TOES, IT'S NOT MANLY!
YOU'RE THE ONE WHOSE BAG MATCHES HIS BELT.
HOW DID YOU FIND ME?
WELL, A CRAZY KING TOLD ME I HAD TO FIND AN EARTHBENDER WHO LISTENS TO THE EARTH.
AND THEN I HAD A VISION IN A MAGIC SWAMP, AND--
WHAT AANG IS TRYING TO SAY IS, HE'S THE AVATAR. AND IF HE DOESN'T MASTER EARTHBENDING SOON, HE WON'T BE ABLE TO DEFEAT THE FIRE LORD.
NOT MY PROBLEM. NOW GET OUT OF HERE, OR I'LL CALL THE GUARDS.
LOOK, WE ALL HAVE TO DO OUR PART TO WIN THIS WAR, AND YOURS IS TO TEACH AANG EARTHBENDING.
GUARDS! GUARDS, HELP!

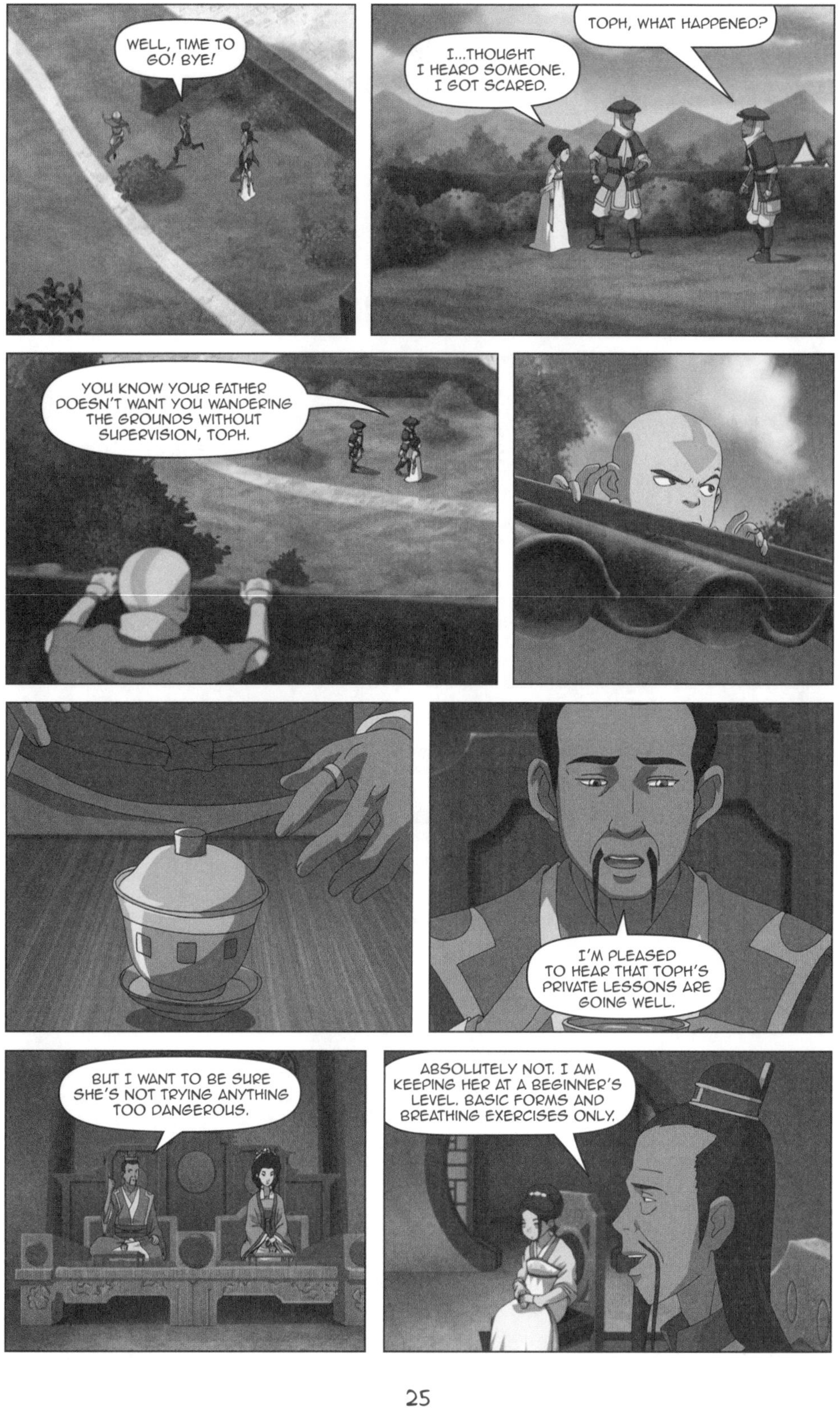

WELL, TIME TO GO! BYE!
TOPH, WHAT HAPPENED?
I...THOUGHT I HEARD SOMEONE. I GOT SCARED.
YOU KNOW YOUR FATHER DOESN'T WANT YOU WANDERING THE GROUNDS WITHOUT SUPERVISION, TOPH.
I'M PLEASED TO HEAR THAT TOPH'S PRIVATE LESSONS ARE GOING WELL.
BUT I WANT TO BE SURE SHE'S NOT TRYING ANYTHING TOO DANGEROUS.
ABSOLUTELY NOT. I AM KEEPING HER AT A BEGINNER'S LEVEL. BASIC FORMS AND BREATHING EXERCISES ONLY.

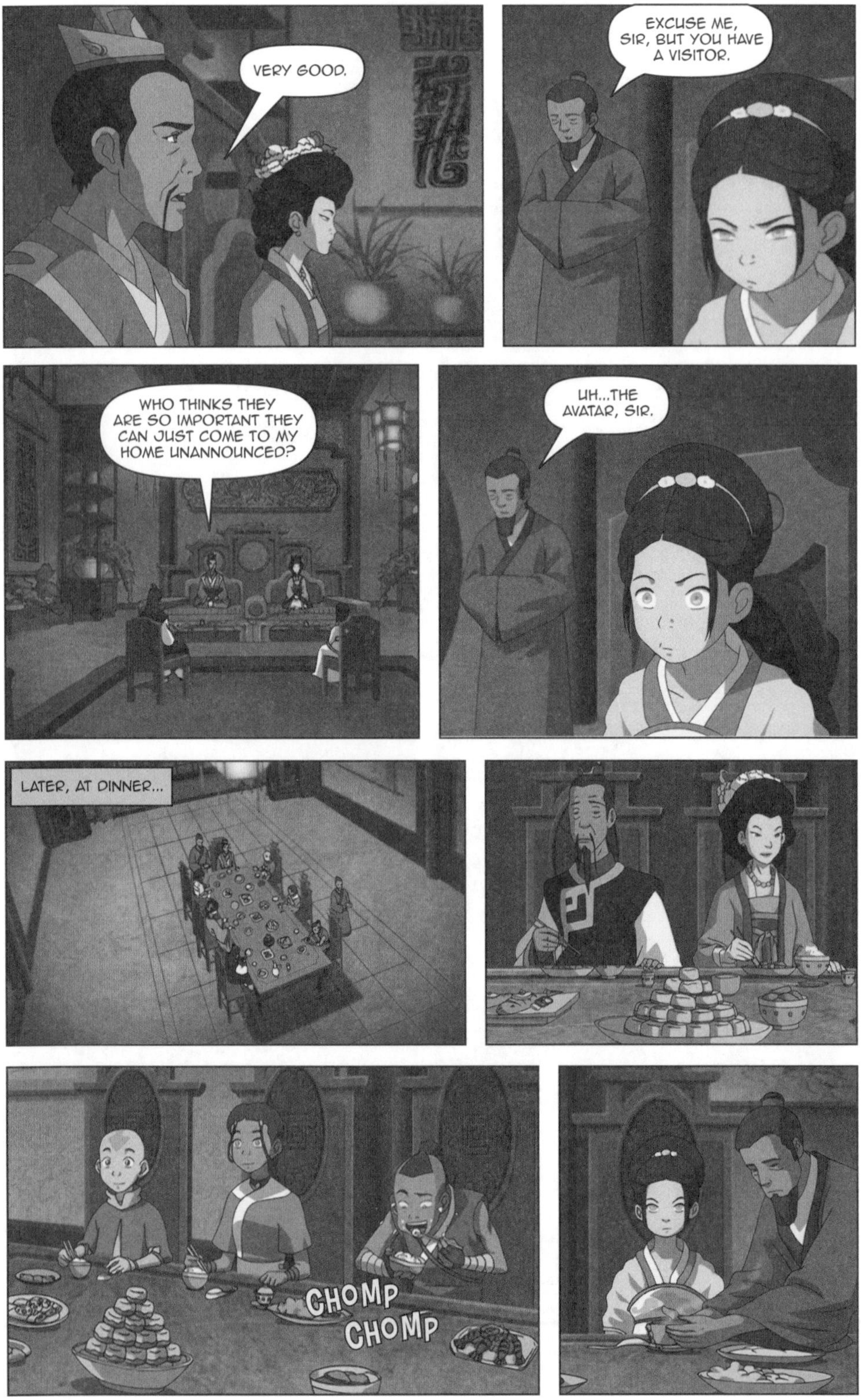
VERY GOOD.
EXCUSE ME, SIR, BUT YOU HAVE A VISITOR.
WHO THINKS THEY ARE SO IMPORTANT THEY CAN JUST COME TO MY HOME UNANNOUNCED?
UH...THE AVATAR, SIR.
LATER, AT DINNER...
CHOMP
CHOMP

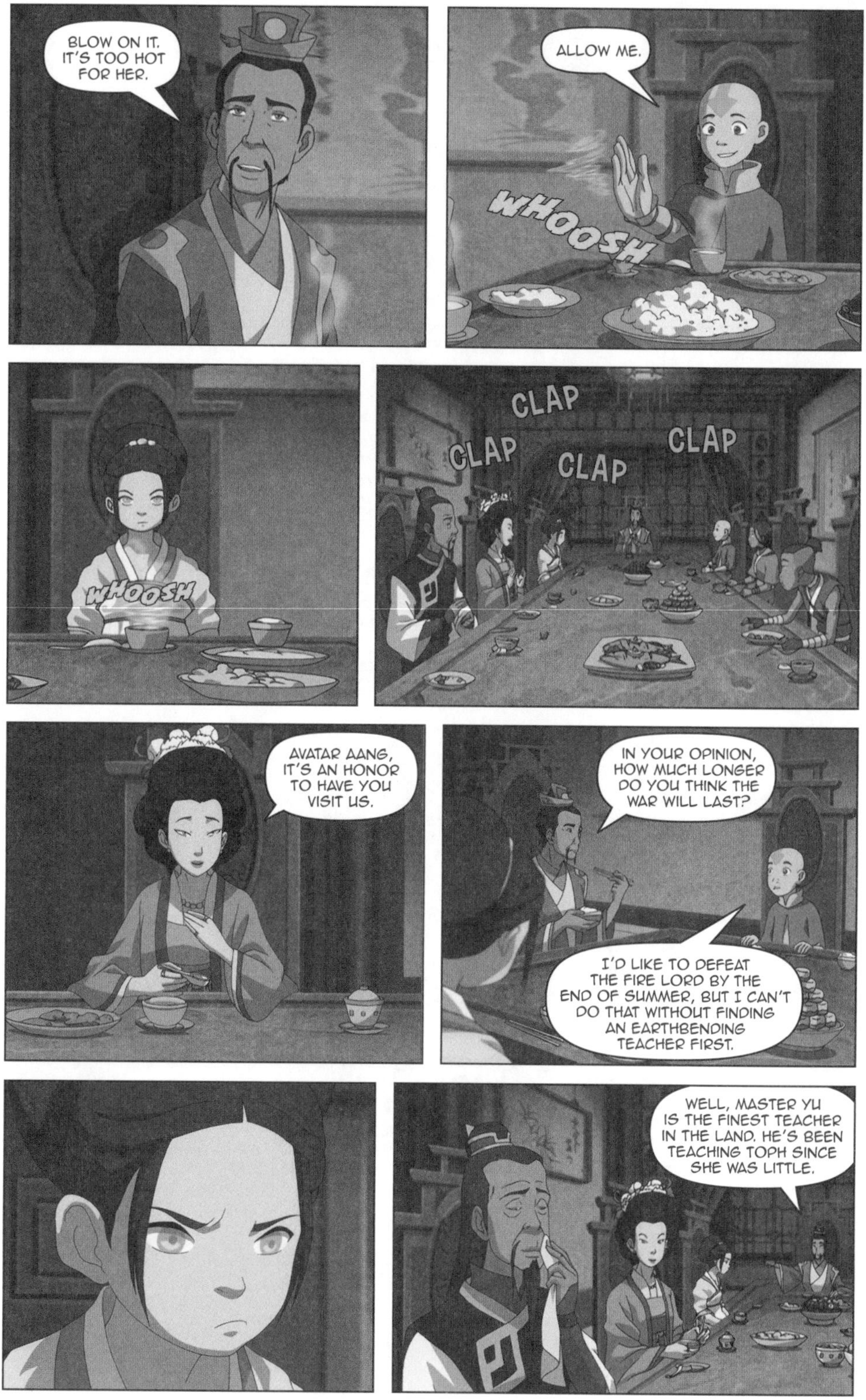
BLOW ON IT. IT'S TOO HOT FOR HER.
ALLOW ME.
WHOOSH
WHOOSH
CLAP
CLAP
CLAP
CLAP
AVATAR AANG, IT'S AN HONOR TO HAVE YOU VISIT US.
IN YOUR OPINION, HOW MUCH LONGER DO YOU THINK THE WAR WILL LAST?
I'D LIKE TO DEFEAT THE FIRE LORD BY THE END OF SUMMER, BUT I CAN'T DO THAT WITHOUT FINDING AN EARTHBENDING TEACHER FIRST.
WELL, MASTER YU IS THE FINEST TEACHER IN THE LAND. HE'S BEEN TEACHING TOPH SINCE SHE WAS LITTLE.

THEN SHE MUST BE A GREAT EARTHBENDER! PROBABLY GOOD ENOUGH TO TEACH SOMEONE ELSE!

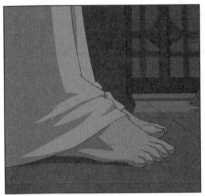

FWOOSH

OW!

TOPH IS STILL LEARNING THE BASICS.

YES, AND SADLY, BECAUSE OF HER BLINDNESS, I DON'T THINK SHE WILL EVER BECOME A TRUE MASTER.

OH, I'M SURE SHE'S BETTER THAN YOU THINK SHE IS.

FWOOSH

SPLOSH

AₐAAA
AₐAAA

CHOO

WHAT'S YOUR PROBLEM?!

WHAT'S *YOUR* PROBLEM?!

WELL, SHALL WE MOVE TO THE LIVING ROOM FOR DESSERT, THEN?

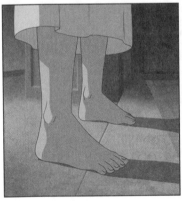
LATER...

GOOD NIGHT, BUDDY.

RELAX. LOOK, I'M SORRY ABOUT DINNER. LET'S CALL A TRUCE, OKAY?

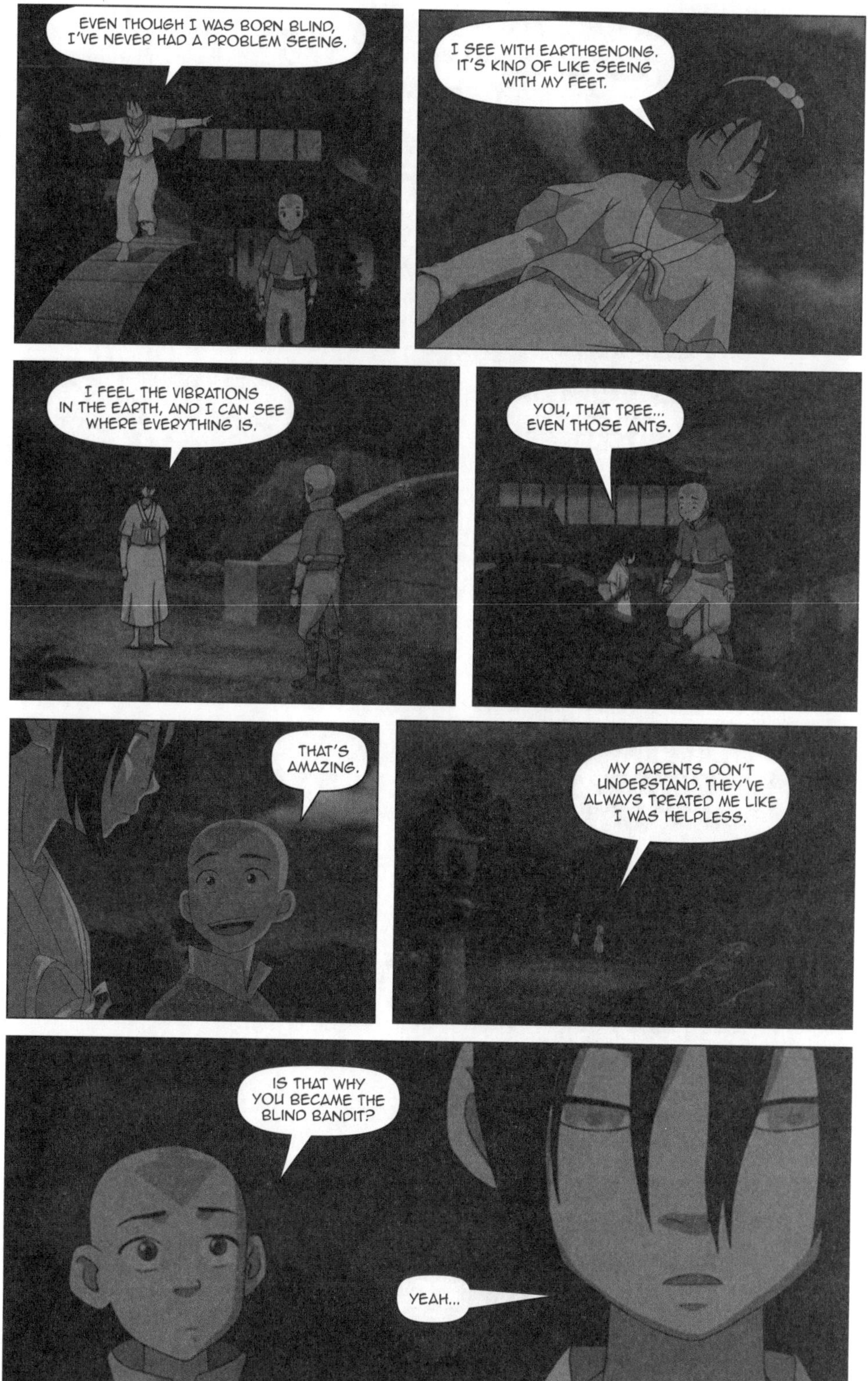
EVEN THOUGH I WAS BORN BLIND, I'VE NEVER HAD A PROBLEM SEEING.
I SEE WITH EARTHBENDING. IT'S KIND OF LIKE SEEING WITH MY FEET.
I FEEL THE VIBRATIONS IN THE EARTH, AND I CAN SEE WHERE EVERYTHING IS.
YOU, THAT TREE... EVEN THOSE ANTS.
THAT'S AMAZING.
MY PARENTS DON'T UNDERSTAND. THEY'VE ALWAYS TREATED ME LIKE I WAS HELPLESS.
IS THAT WHY YOU BECAME THE BLIND BANDIT?
YEAH...

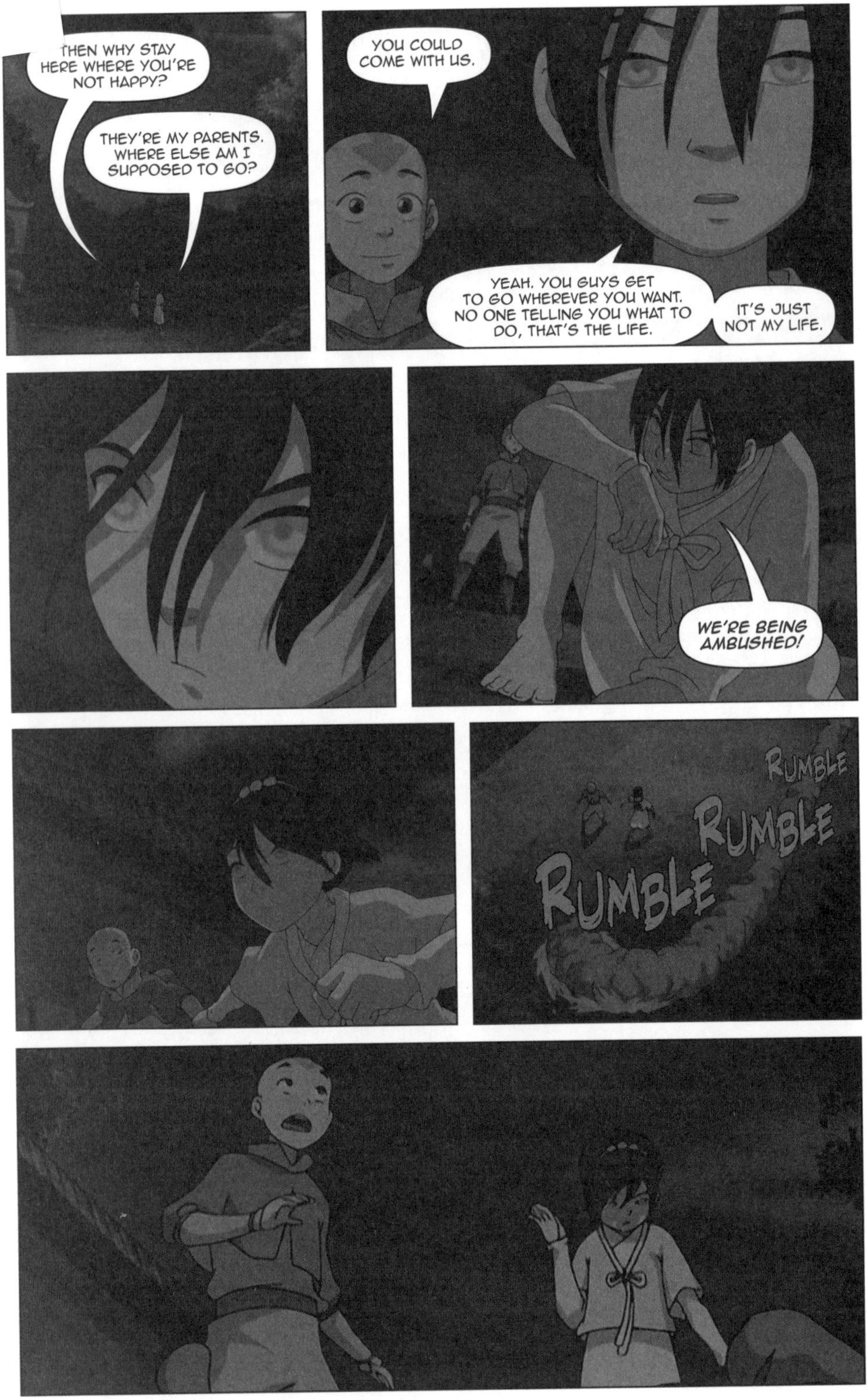
THEN WHY STAY HERE WHERE YOU'RE NOT HAPPY?
THEY'RE MY PARENTS. WHERE ELSE AM I SUPPOSED TO GO?
YOU COULD COME WITH US.
YEAH. YOU GUYS GET TO GO WHEREVER YOU WANT. NO ONE TELLING YOU WHAT TO DO, THAT'S THE LIFE.
IT'S JUST NOT MY LIFE.
WE'RE BEING AMBUSHED!
RUMBLE
RUMBLE
RUMBLE

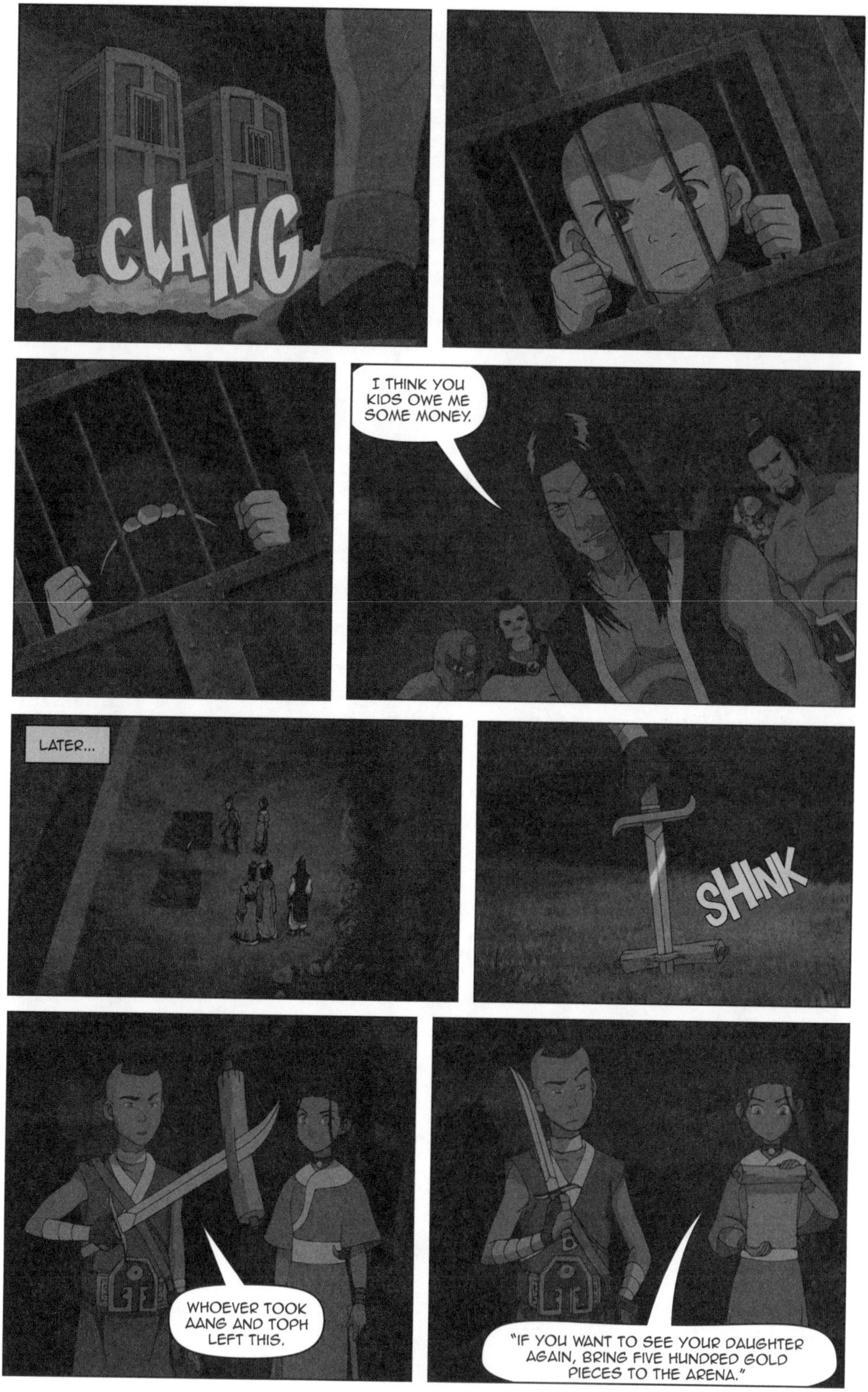
CLANG
I THINK YOU KIDS OWE ME SOME MONEY.
LATER...
SHINK
WHOEVER TOOK AANG AND TOPH LEFT THIS.
"IF YOU WANT TO SEE YOUR DAUGHTER AGAIN, BRING FIVE HUNDRED GOLD PIECES TO THE ARENA."

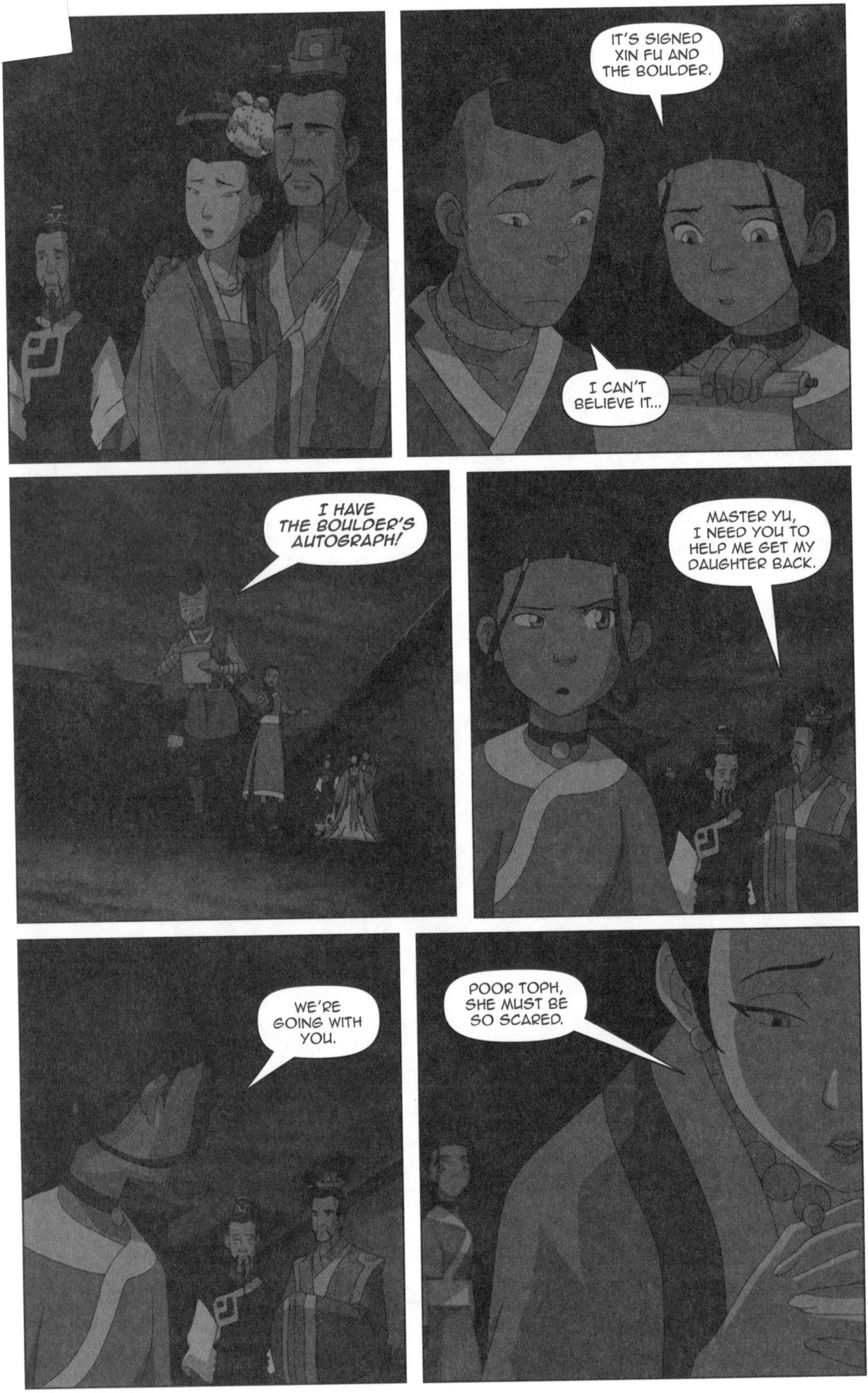
IT'S SIGNED XIN FU AND THE BOULDER.
I CAN'T BELIEVE IT...
I HAVE THE BOULDER'S AUTOGRAPH!
MASTER YU, I NEED YOU TO HELP ME GET MY DAUGHTER BACK.
WE'RE GOING WITH YOU.
POOR TOPH, SHE MUST BE SO SCARED.

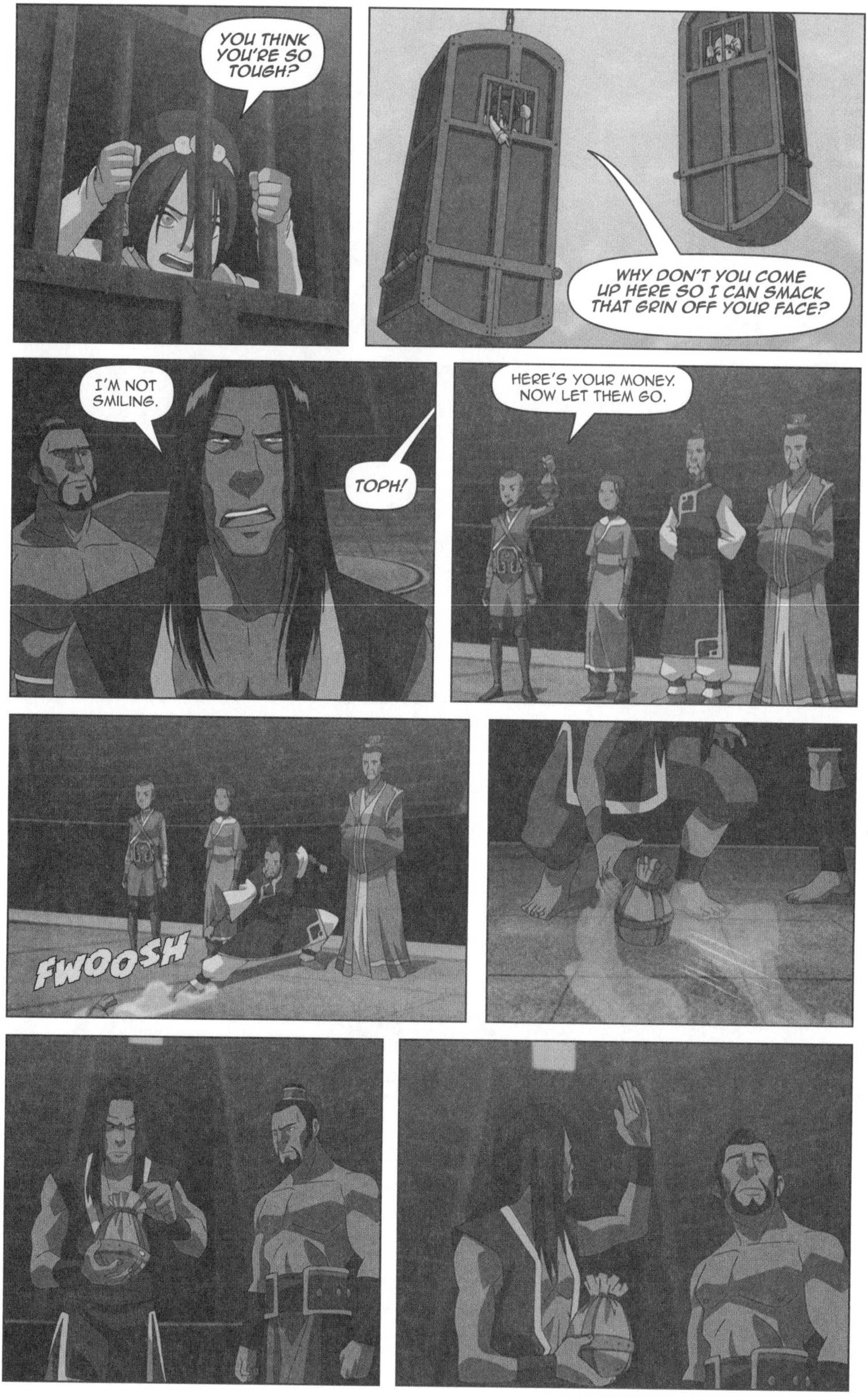
YOU THINK YOU'RE SO TOUGH?
WHY DON'T YOU COME UP HERE SO I CAN SMACK THAT GRIN OFF YOUR FACE?
I'M NOT SMILING.
TOPH!
HERE'S YOUR MONEY. NOW LET THEM GO.
FWOOSH

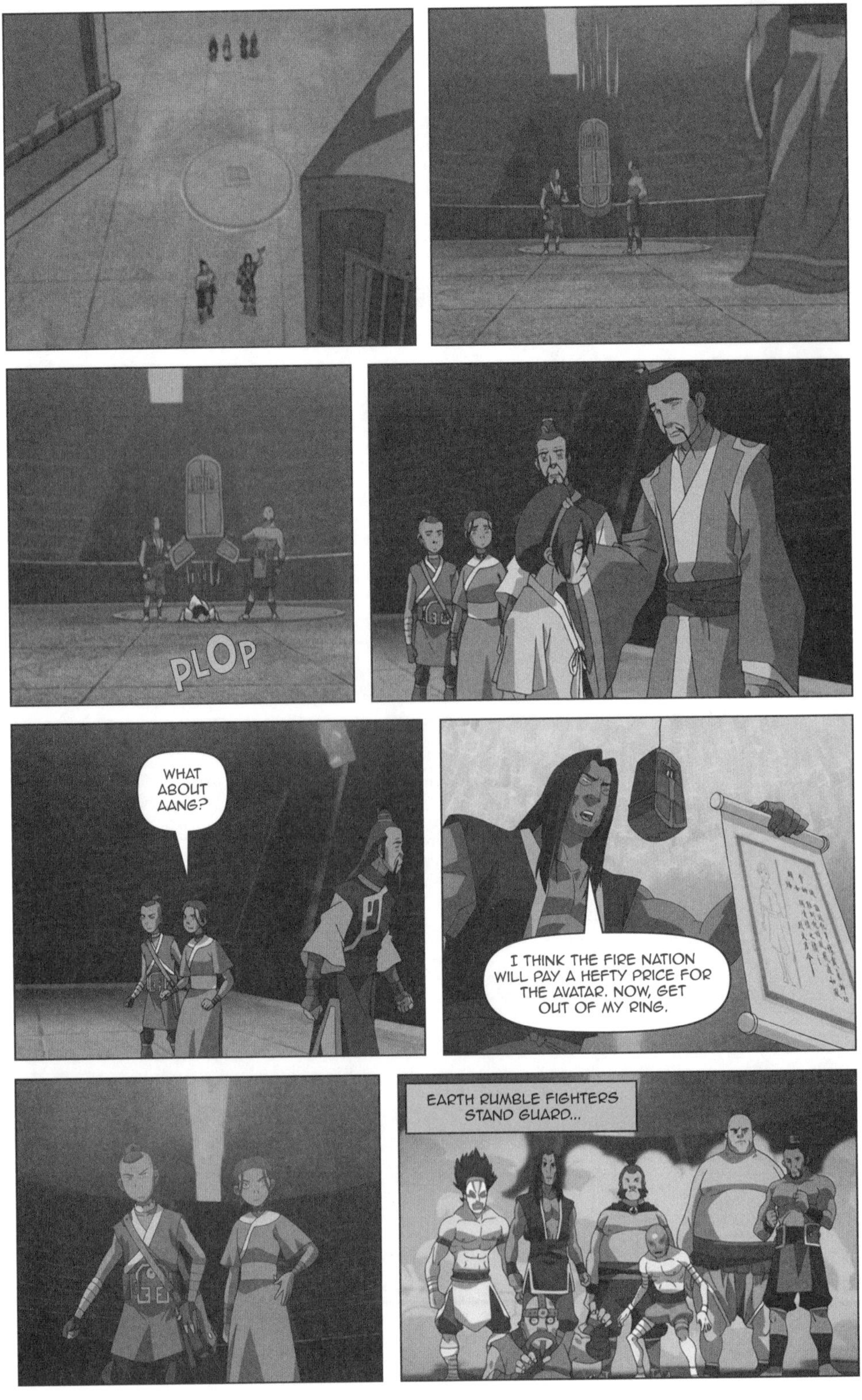
PLOP
WHAT ABOUT AANG?
I THINK THE FIRE NATION WILL PAY A HEFTY PRICE FOR THE AVATAR. NOW, GET OUT OF MY RING.
EARTH RUMBLE FIGHTERS STAND GUARD...

GO, I'LL BE OKAY.

TOPH, THERE'S TOO MANY OF THEM. WE NEED AN EARTHBENDER. WE NEED YOU!

MY DAUGHTER IS BLIND. SHE IS BLIND AND TINY AND HELPLESS AND FRAGILE. SHE CANNOT HELP YOU!

YES, I CAN.

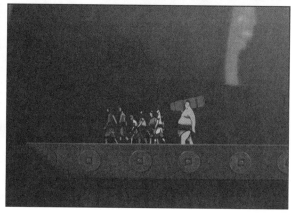

LET HIM GO! I BEAT YOU ALL BEFORE, AND I'LL DO IT AGAIN!

THE BOULDER TAKES ISSUE WITH THAT COMMENT.

WAIT!

TRAMP
TRAMP
TRAMP

THEY'RE MINE.

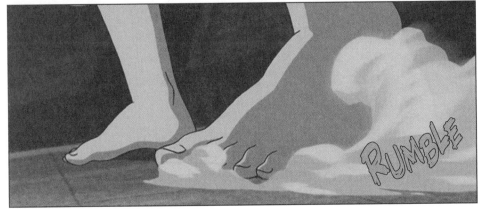

RUMBLE

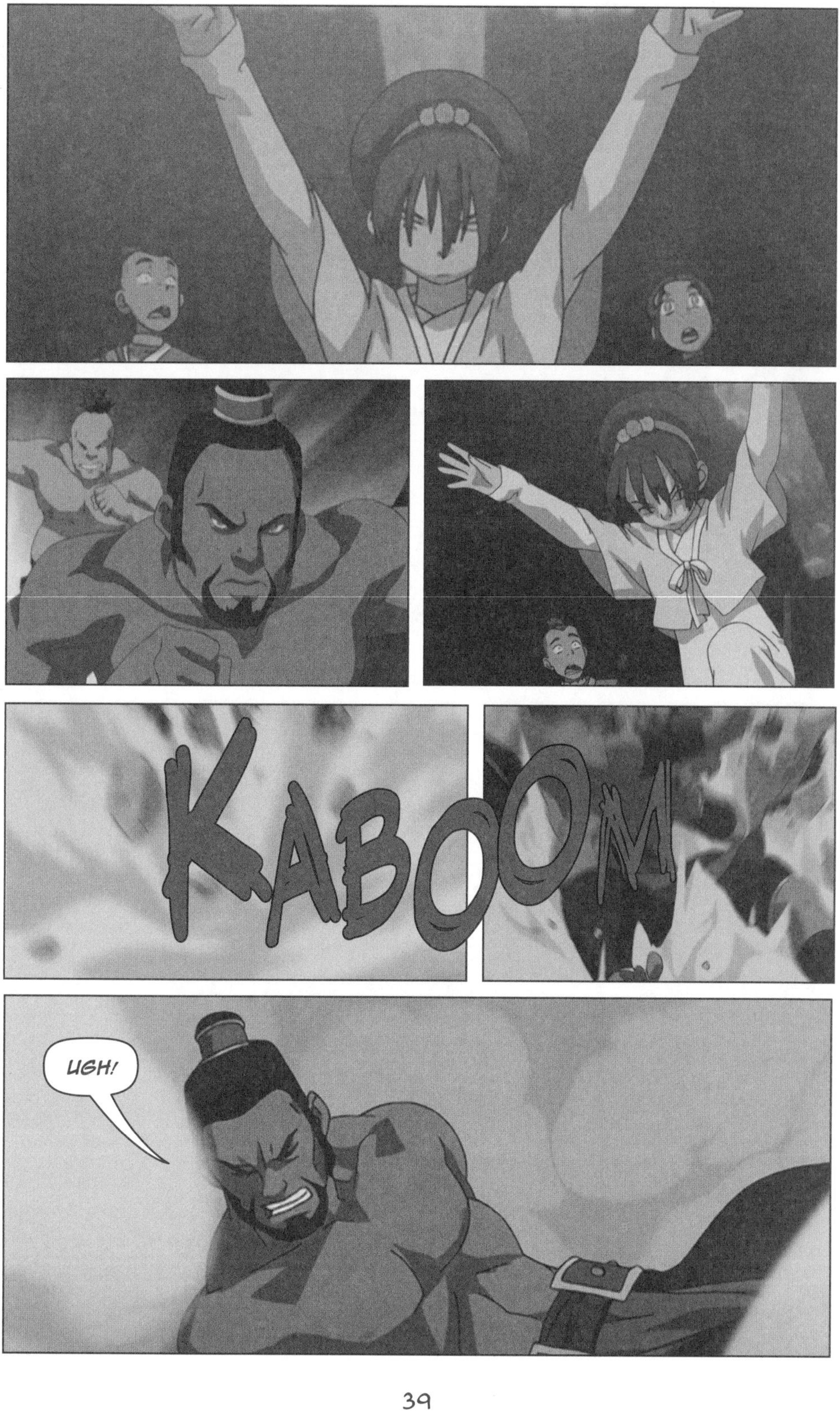
KABOOM
UGH!

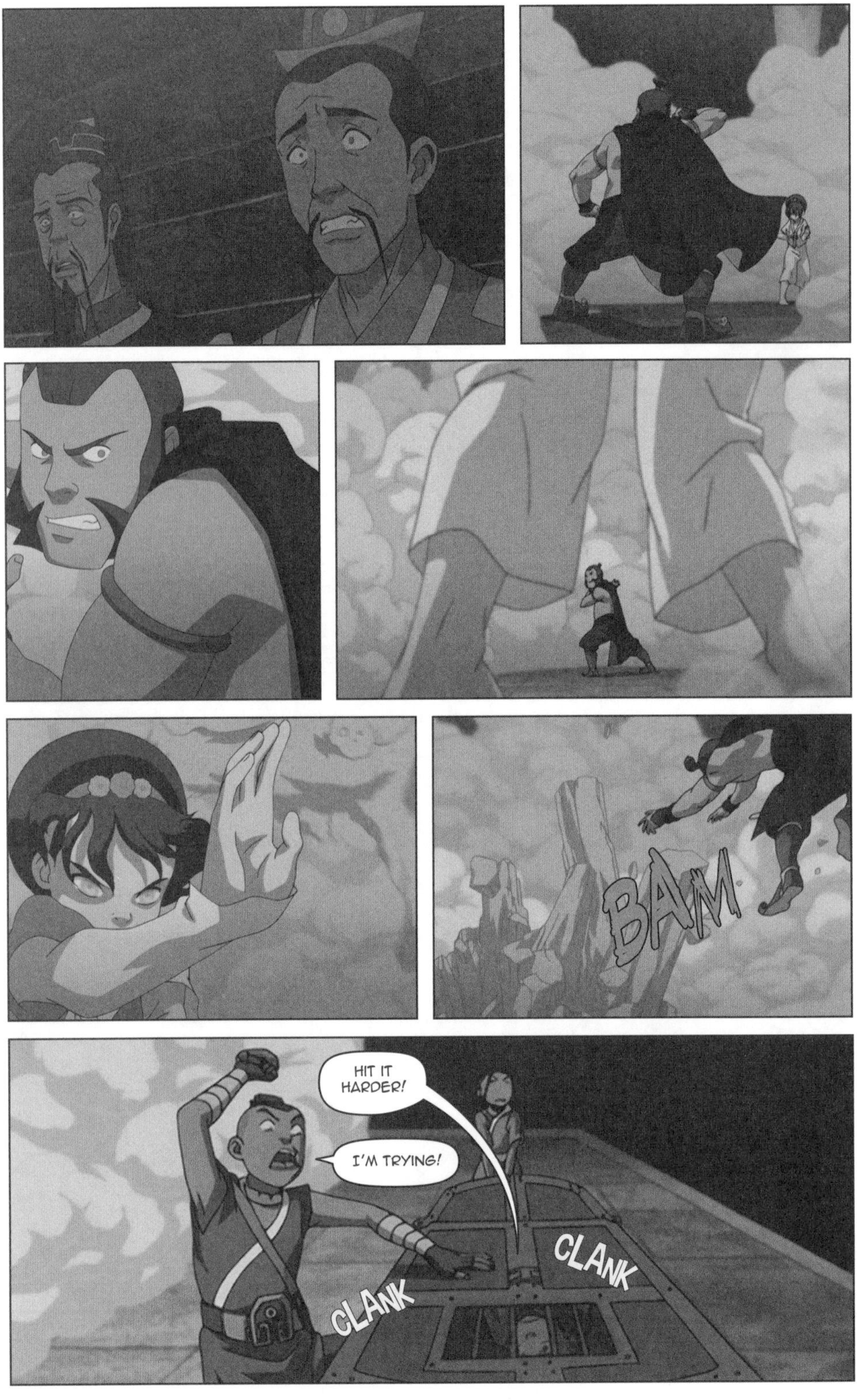
BAM
HIT IT HARDER!
I'M TRYING!
CLANK
CLANK

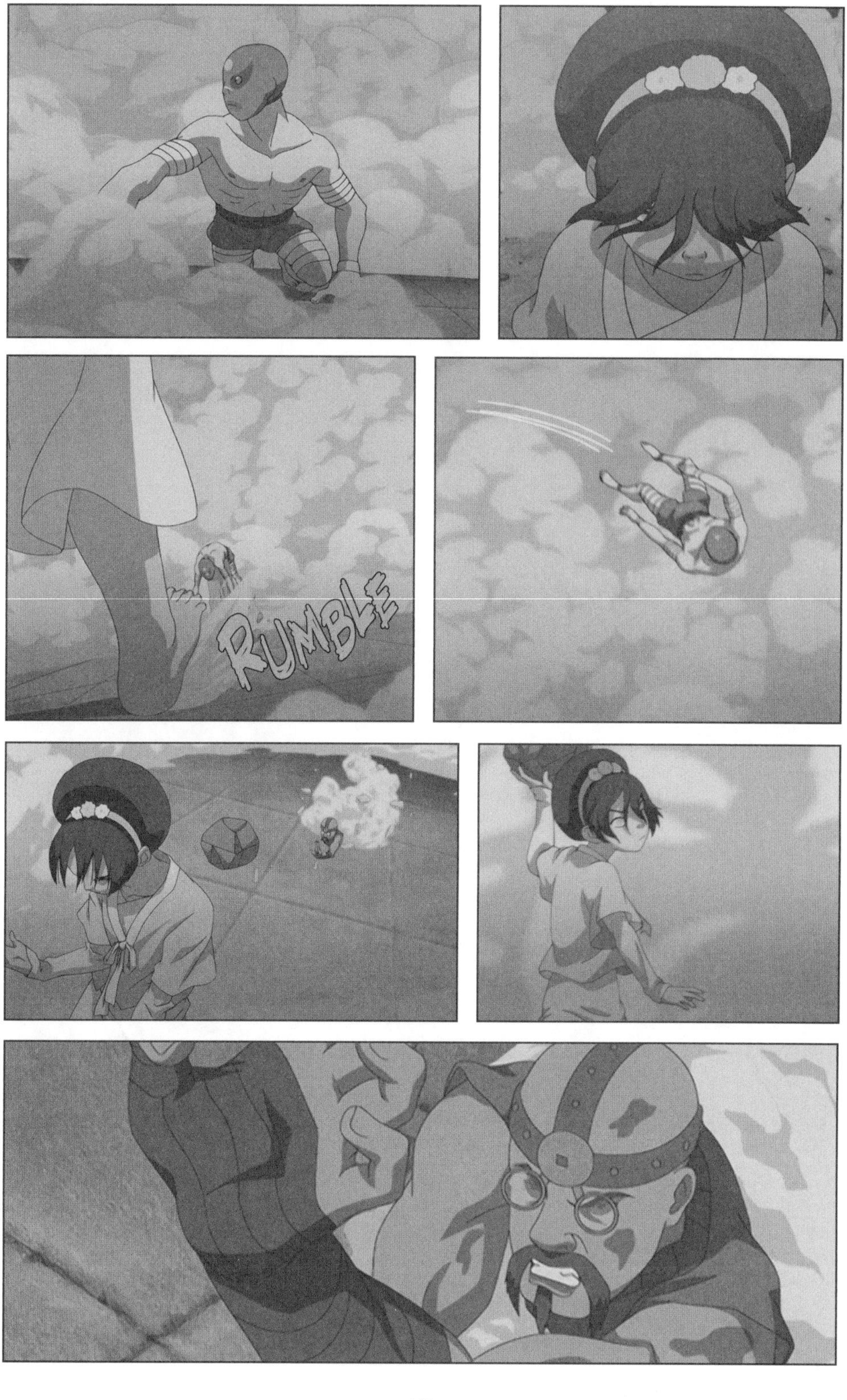
RUMBLE

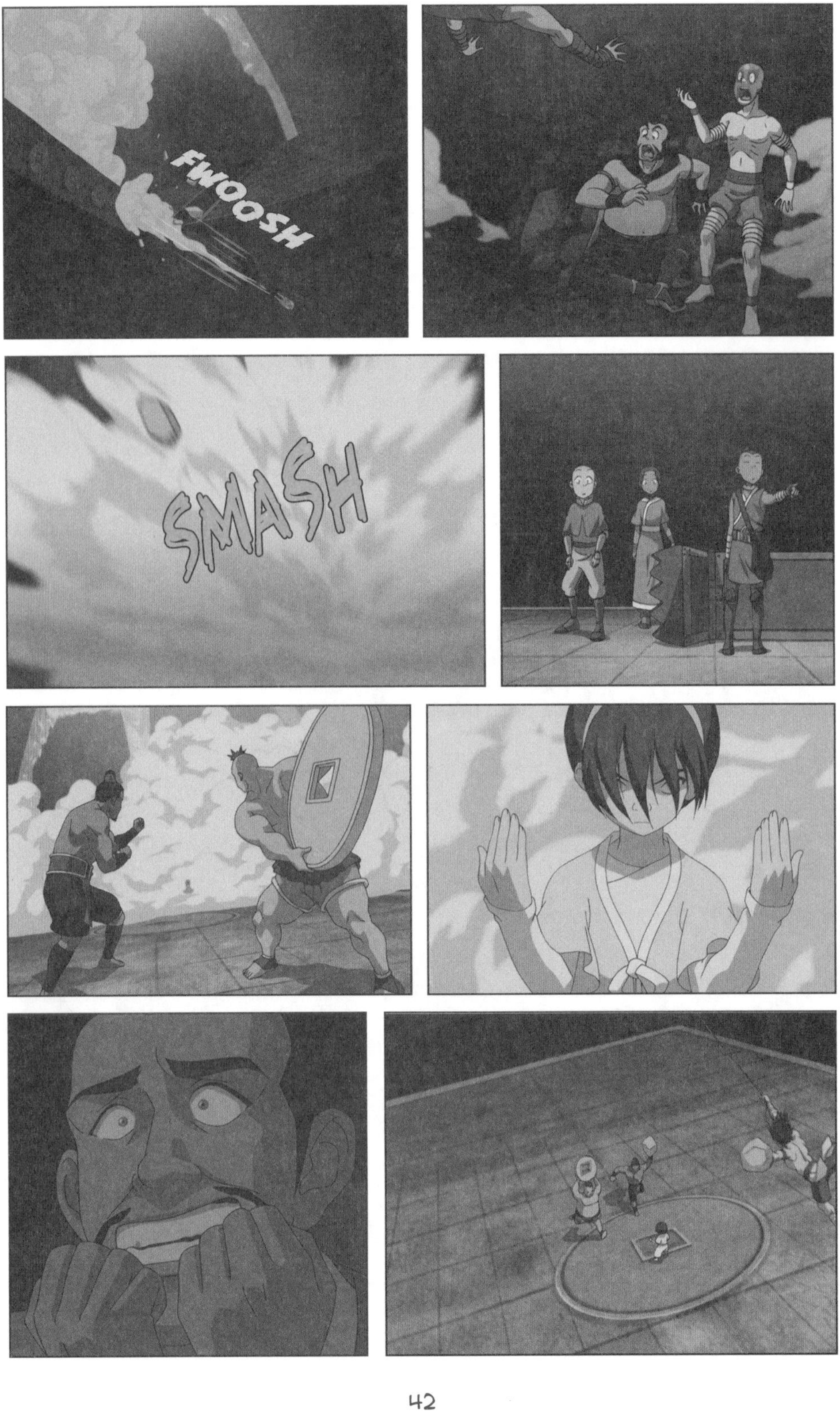
FWOOSH
SMASH

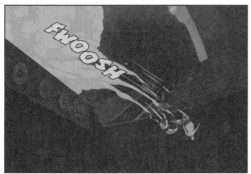

I NEVER KNEW. YOUR DAUGHTER'S AMAZING!

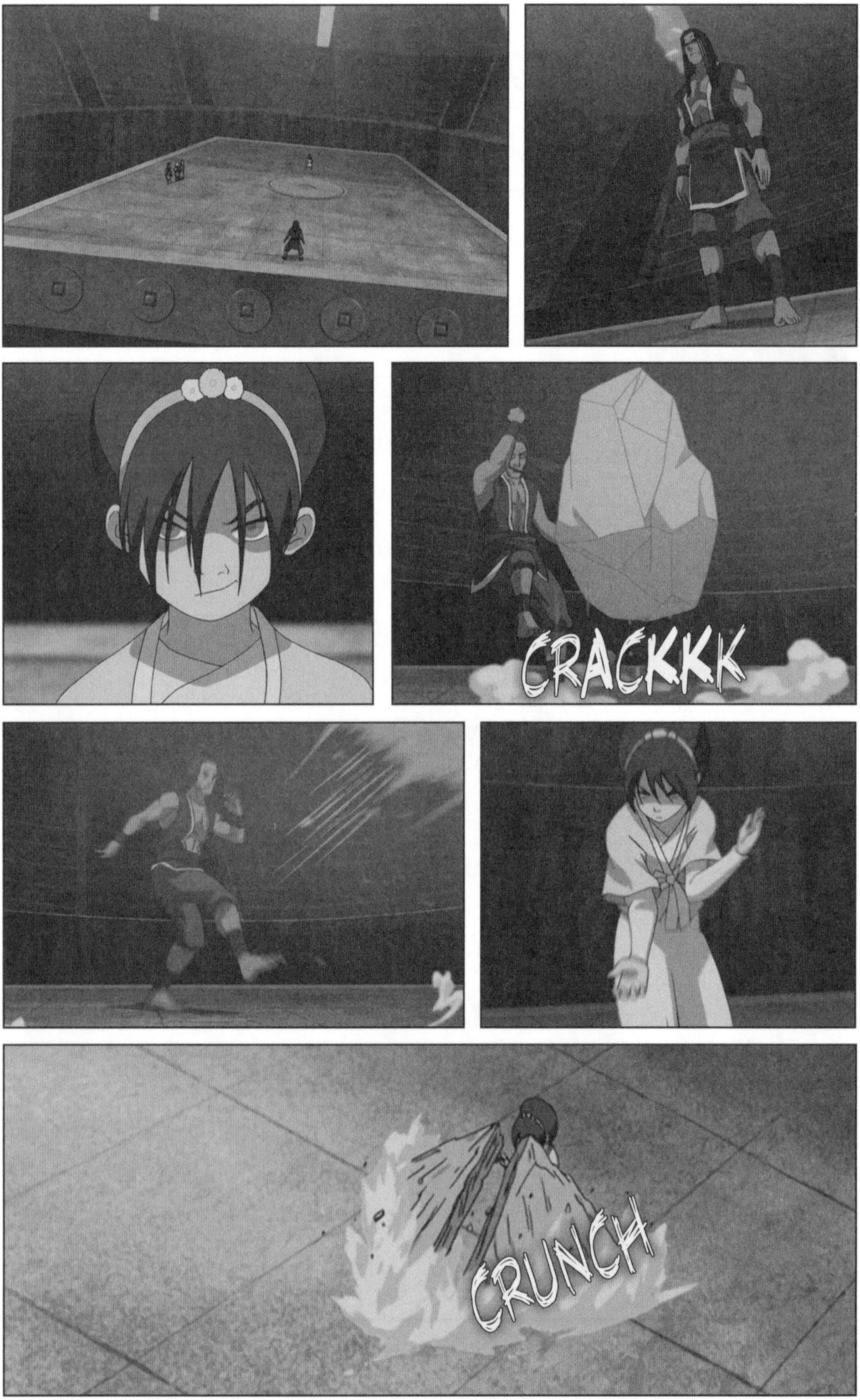
CRACKKK
CRUNCH

WHACKKK

RUMBLE

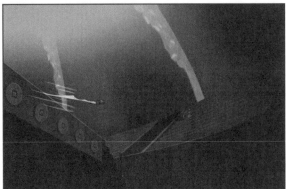

SLAM

SHE'S THE GREATEST EARTHBENDER I'VE EVER SEEN.

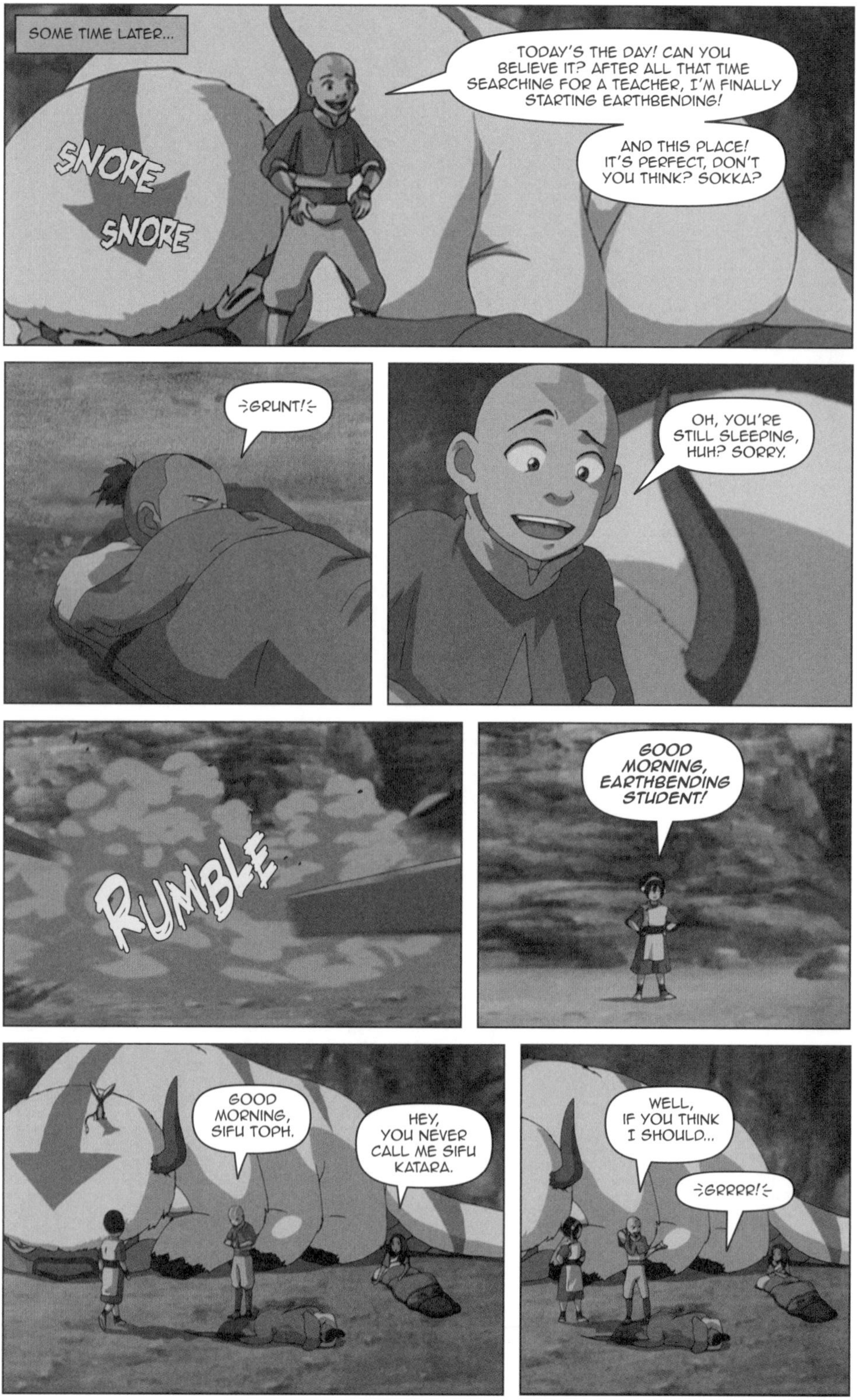
SOME TIME LATER...
TODAY'S THE DAY! CAN YOU BELIEVE IT? AFTER ALL THAT TIME SEARCHING FOR A TEACHER, I'M FINALLY STARTING EARTHBENDING!
AND THIS PLACE! IT'S PERFECT, DON'T YOU THINK? SOKKA?
SNORE
SNORE
GRUNT!
OH, YOU'RE STILL SLEEPING, HUH? SORRY.
RUMBLE
GOOD MORNING, EARTHBENDING STUDENT!
GOOD MORNING, SIFU TOPH.
HEY, YOU NEVER CALL ME SIFU KATARA.
WELL, IF YOU THINK I SHOULD...
GRRRR!

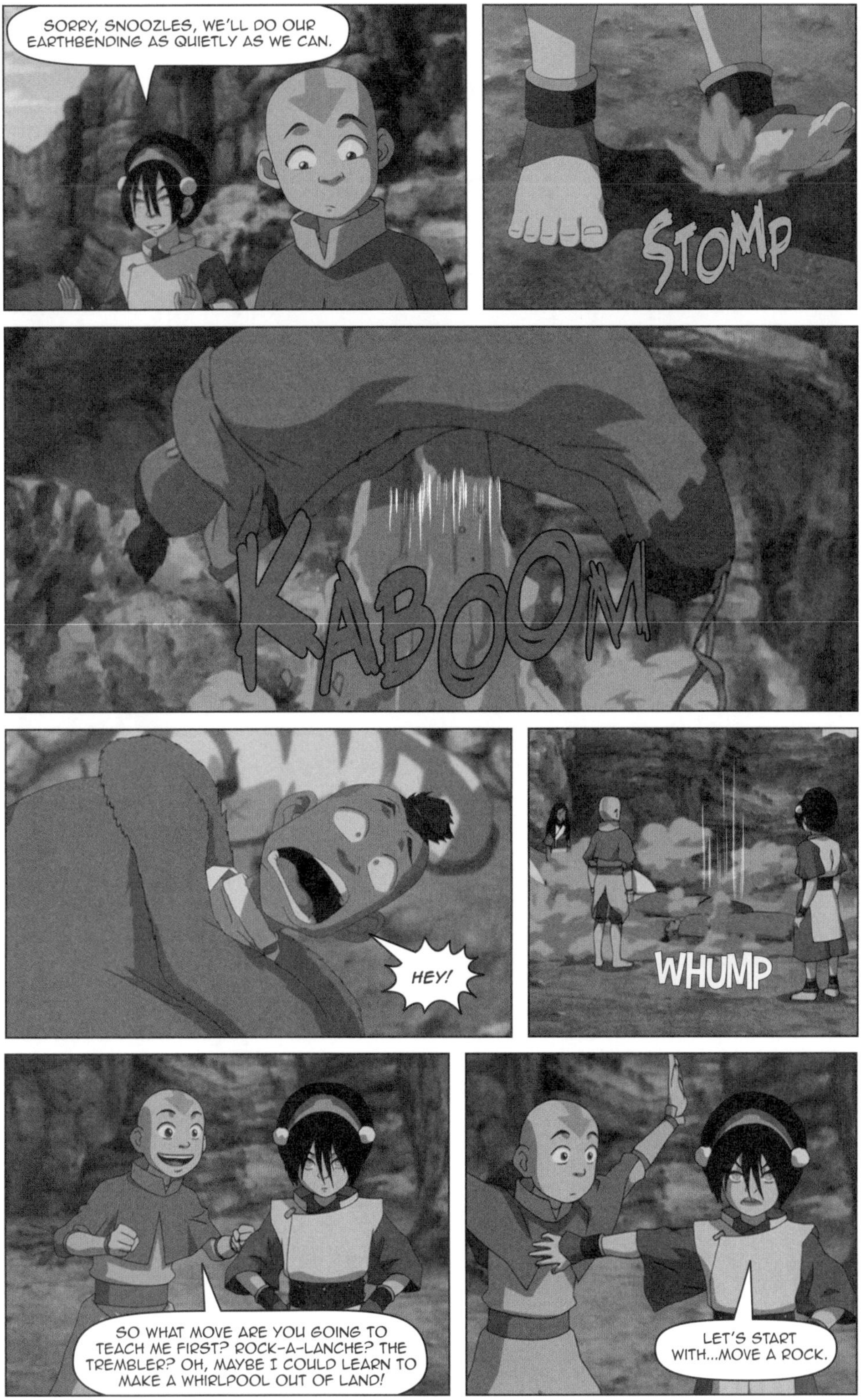
SORRY, SNOOZLES, WE'LL DO OUR EARTHBENDING AS QUIETLY AS WE CAN.
STOMP
KABOOM
HEY!
WHUMP
SO WHAT MOVE ARE YOU GOING TO TEACH ME FIRST? ROCK-A-LANCHE? THE TREMBLER? OH, MAYBE I COULD LEARN TO MAKE A WHIRLPOOL OUT OF LAND!
LET'S START WITH...MOVE A ROCK.

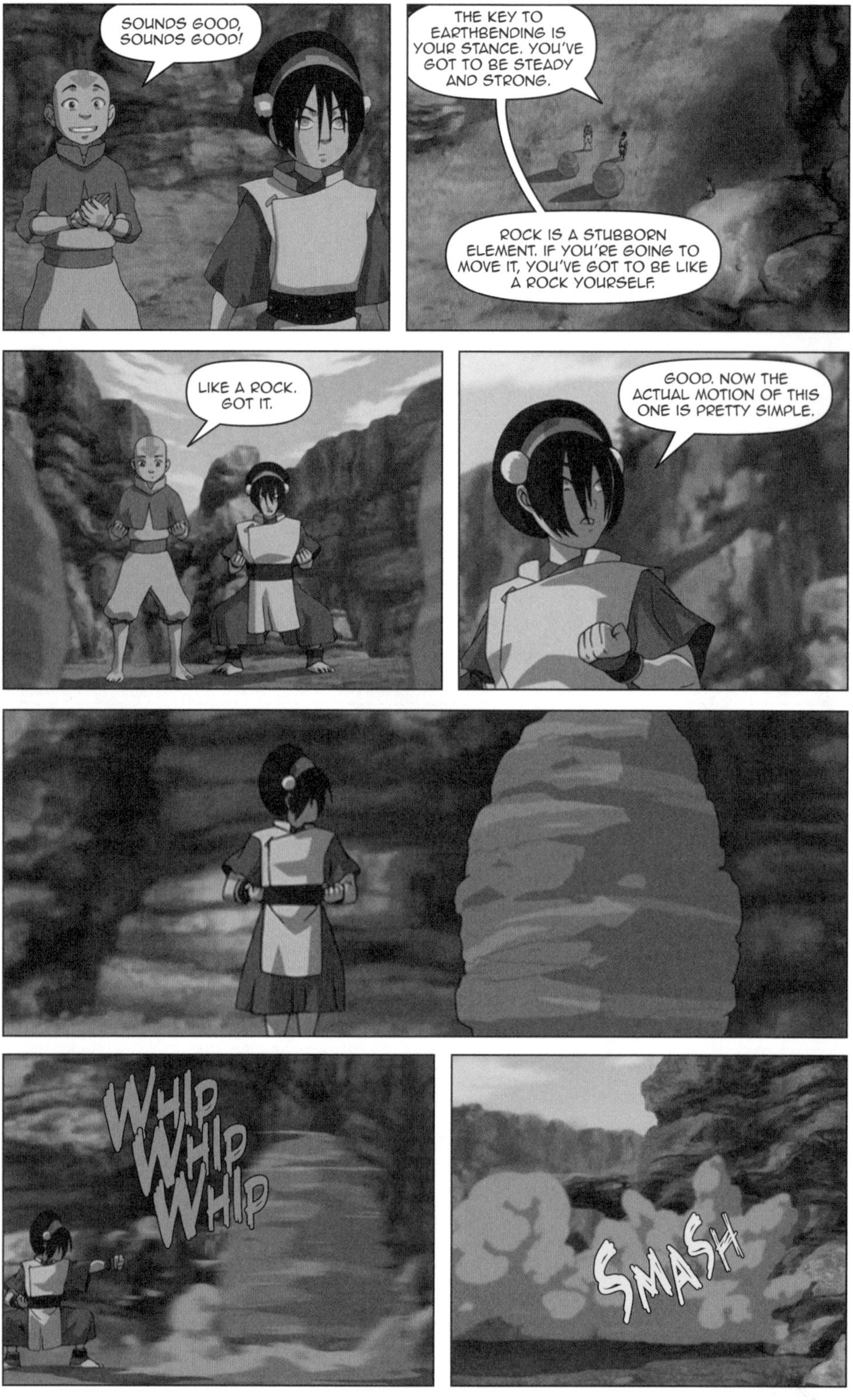
SOUNDS GOOD, SOUNDS GOOD!
THE KEY TO EARTHBENDING IS YOUR STANCE. YOU'VE GOT TO BE STEADY AND STRONG.
ROCK IS A STUBBORN ELEMENT. IF YOU'RE GOING TO MOVE IT, YOU'VE GOT TO BE LIKE A ROCK YOURSELF.
LIKE A ROCK. GOT IT.
GOOD. NOW THE ACTUAL MOTION OF THIS ONE IS PRETTY SIMPLE.
WHIP WHIP WHIP
SMASH

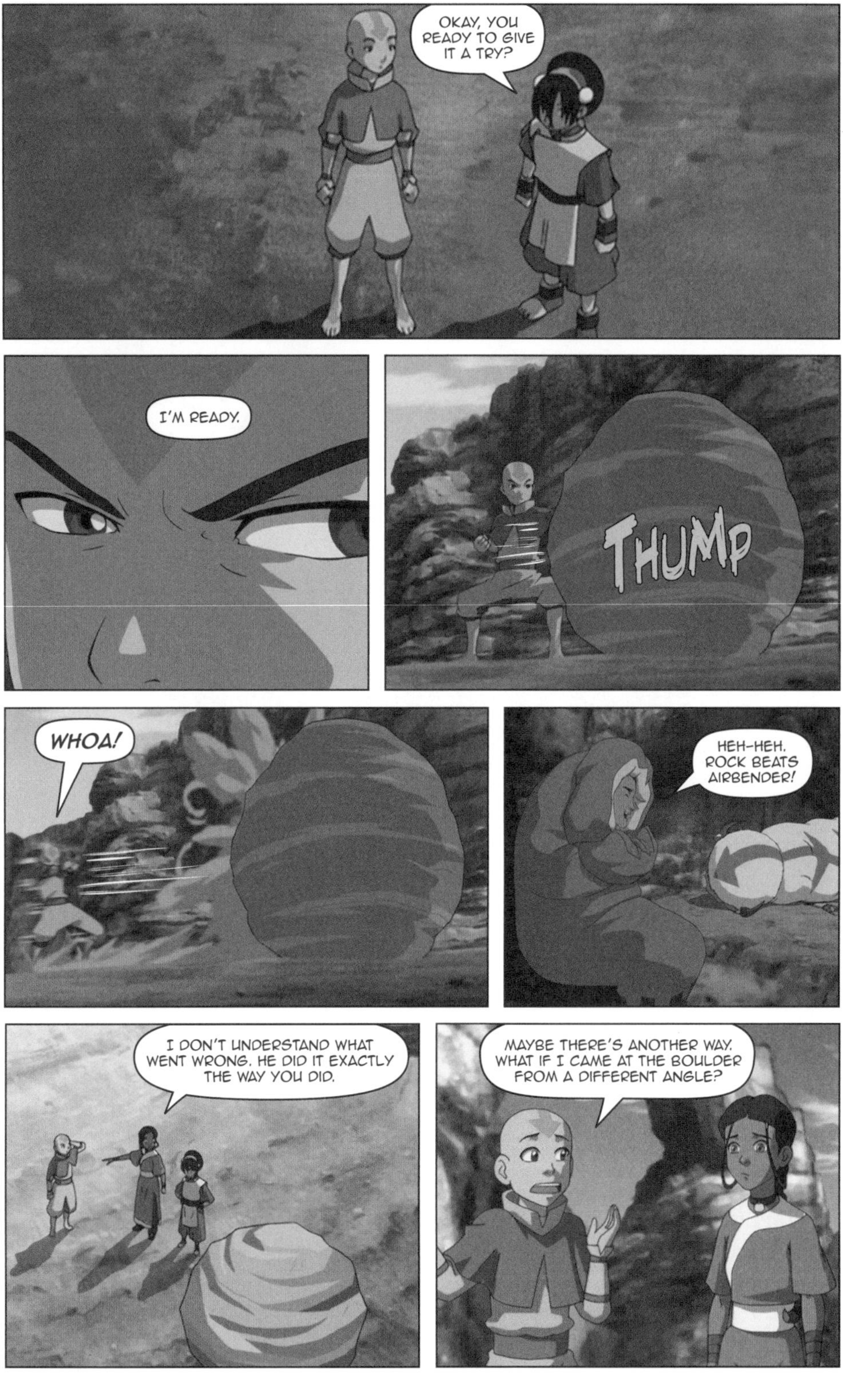
OKAY, YOU READY TO GIVE IT A TRY?
I'M READY.
THUMP
WHOA!
HEH-HEH. ROCK BEATS AIRBENDER!
I DON'T UNDERSTAND WHAT WENT WRONG. HE DID IT EXACTLY THE WAY YOU DID.
MAYBE THERE'S ANOTHER WAY. WHAT IF I CAME AT THE BOULDER FROM A DIFFERENT ANGLE?

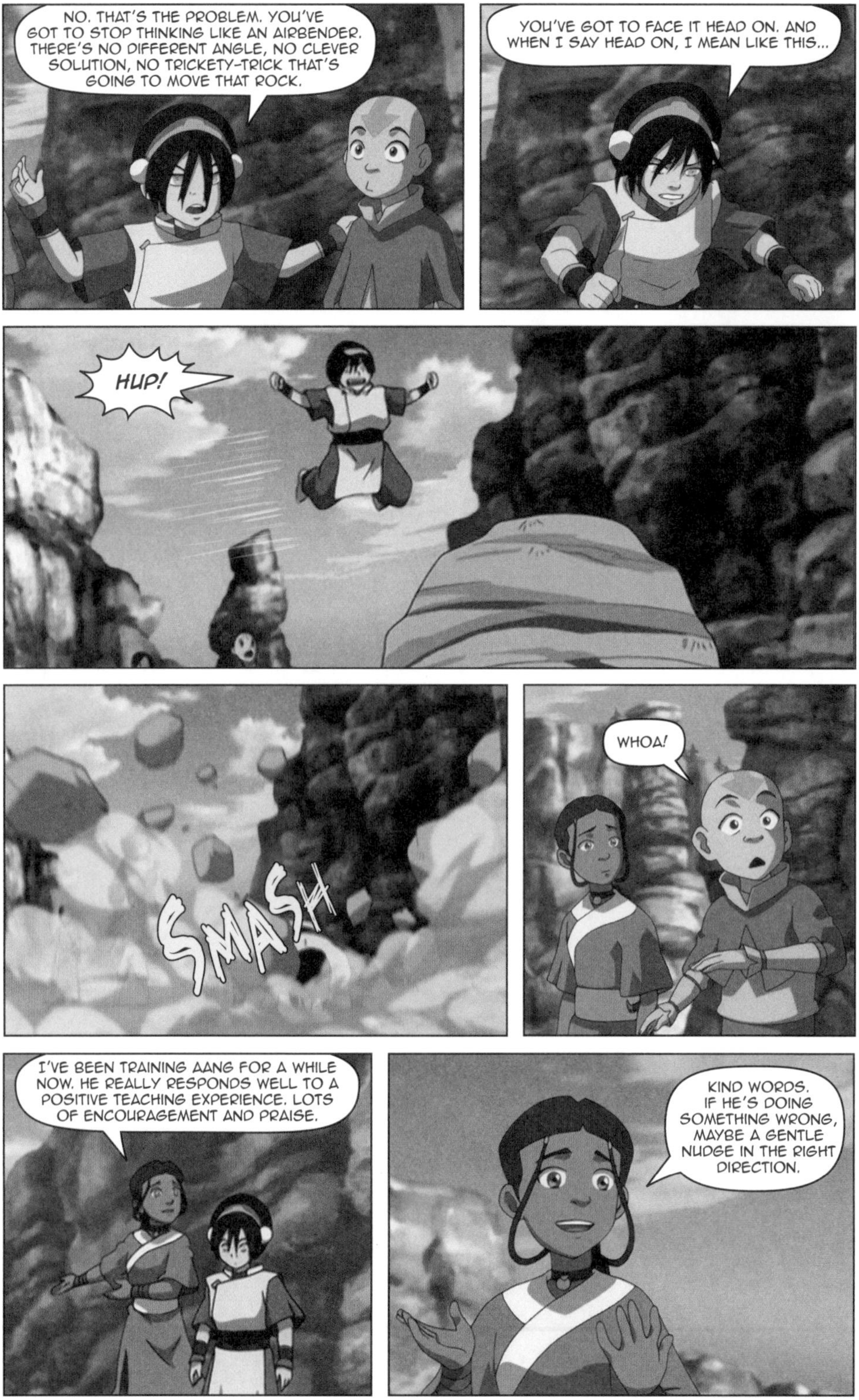
NO. THAT'S THE PROBLEM. YOU'VE GOT TO STOP THINKING LIKE AN AIRBENDER. THERE'S NO DIFFERENT ANGLE, NO CLEVER SOLUTION, NO TRICKETY-TRICK THAT'S GOING TO MOVE THAT ROCK.
YOU'VE GOT TO FACE IT HEAD ON. AND WHEN I SAY HEAD ON, I MEAN LIKE THIS...
HUP!
SMASH
WHOA!
I'VE BEEN TRAINING AANG FOR A WHILE NOW. HE REALLY RESPONDS WELL TO A POSITIVE TEACHING EXPERIENCE. LOTS OF ENCOURAGEMENT AND PRAISE.
KIND WORDS. IF HE'S DOING SOMETHING WRONG, MAYBE A GENTLE NUDGE IN THE RIGHT DIRECTION.

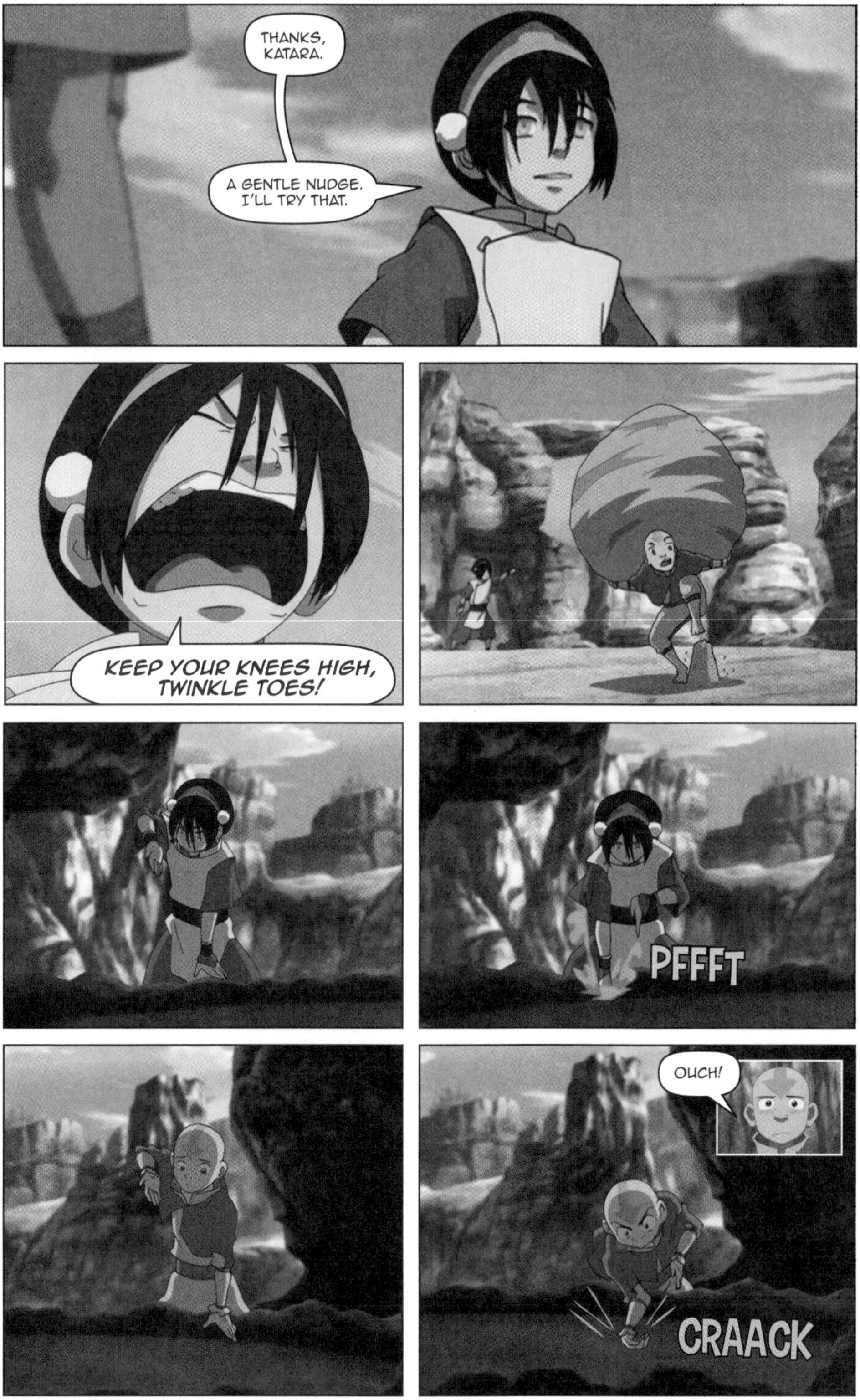
THANKS, KATARA.
A GENTLE NUDGE. I'LL TRY THAT.
KEEP YOUR KNEES HIGH, TWINKLE TOES!
PFFFT
OUCH!
CRAACK

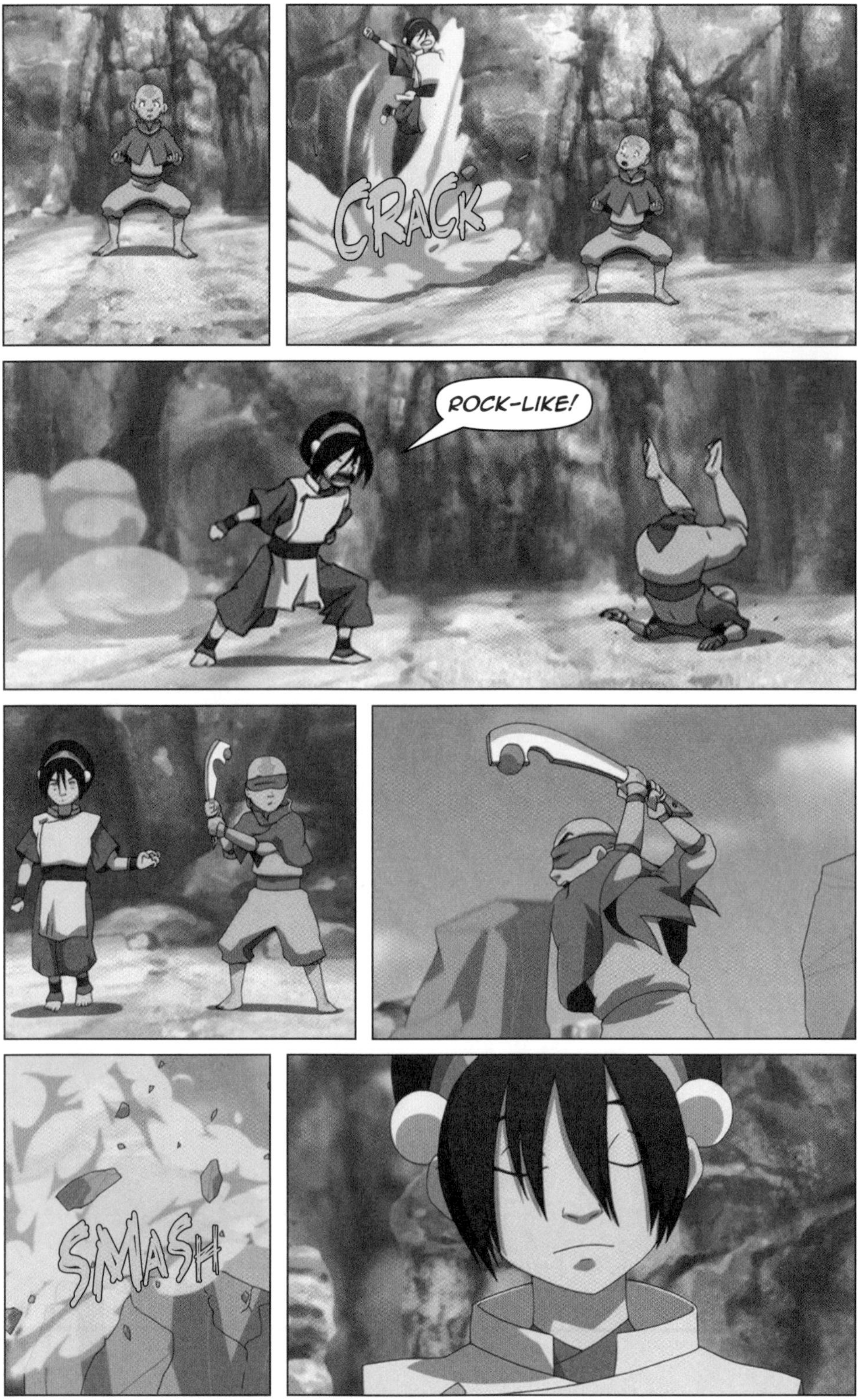
CRACK
ROCK-LIKE!
SMASH

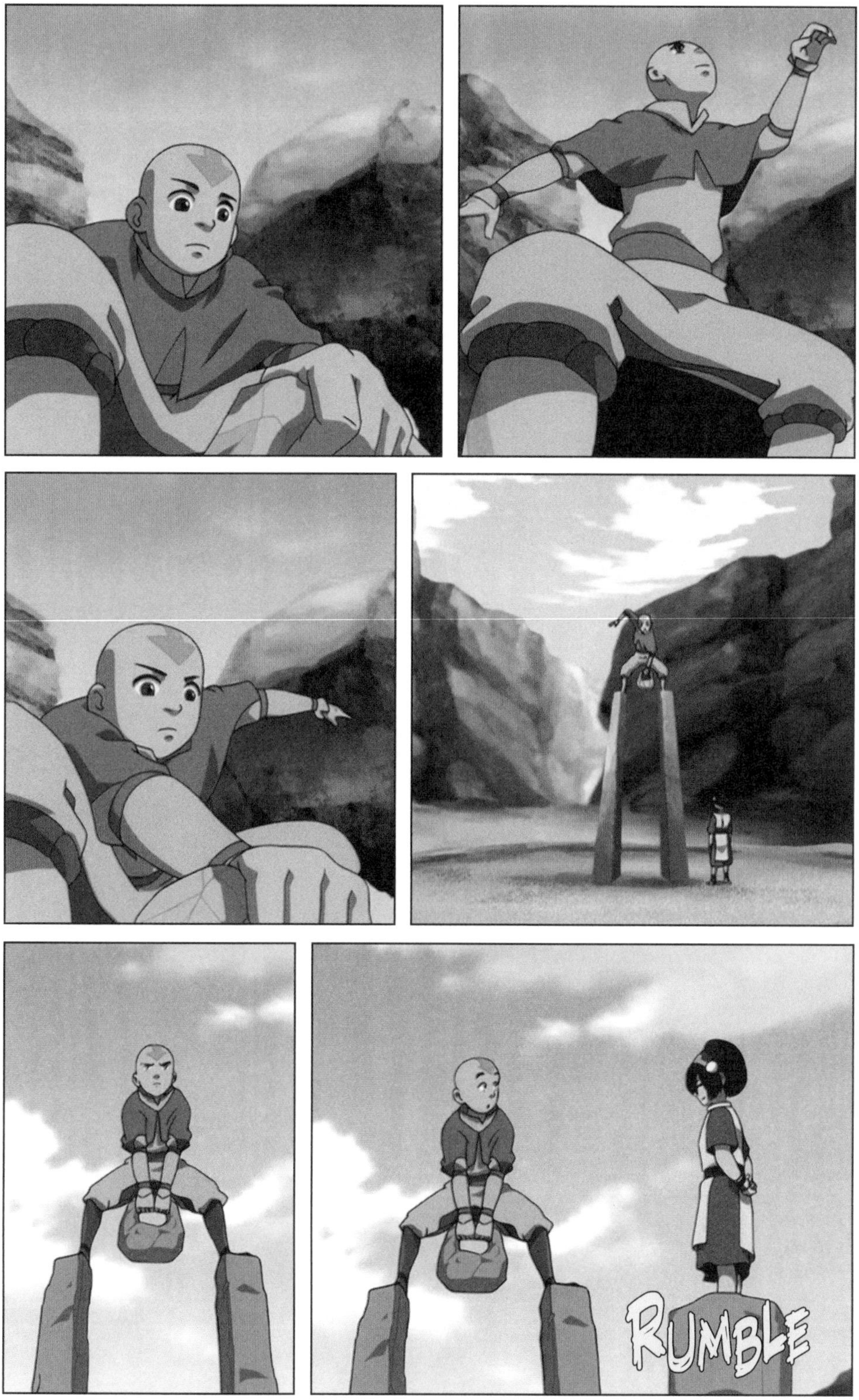
RUMBLE

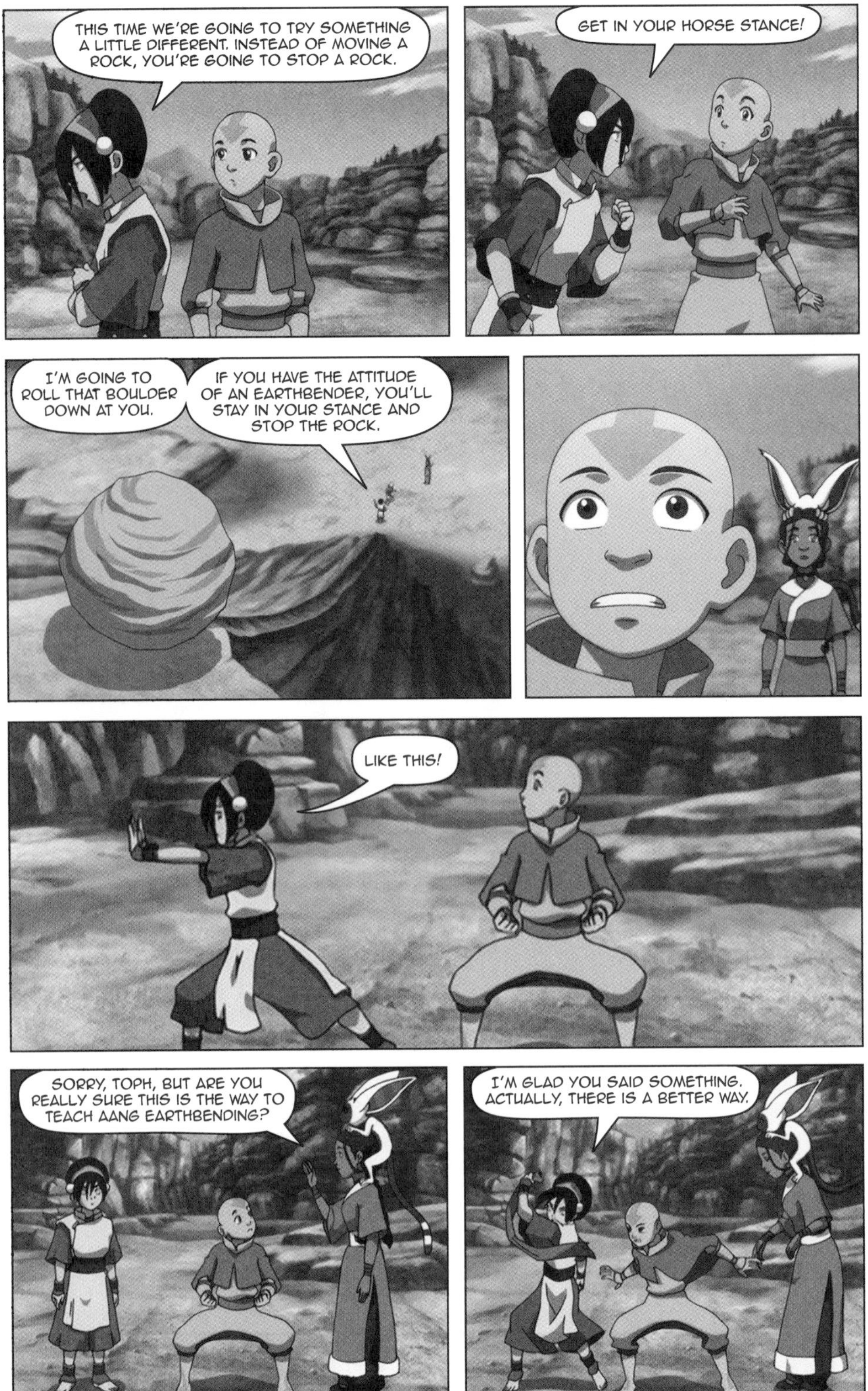
THIS TIME WE'RE GOING TO TRY SOMETHING A LITTLE DIFFERENT. INSTEAD OF MOVING A ROCK, YOU'RE GOING TO STOP A ROCK.
GET IN YOUR HORSE STANCE!
I'M GOING TO ROLL THAT BOULDER DOWN AT YOU.
IF YOU HAVE THE ATTITUDE OF AN EARTHBENDER, YOU'LL STAY IN YOUR STANCE AND STOP THE ROCK.
LIKE THIS!
SORRY, TOPH, BUT ARE YOU REALLY SURE THIS IS THE WAY TO TEACH AANG EARTHBENDING?
I'M GLAD YOU SAID SOMETHING. ACTUALLY, THERE IS A BETTER WAY.

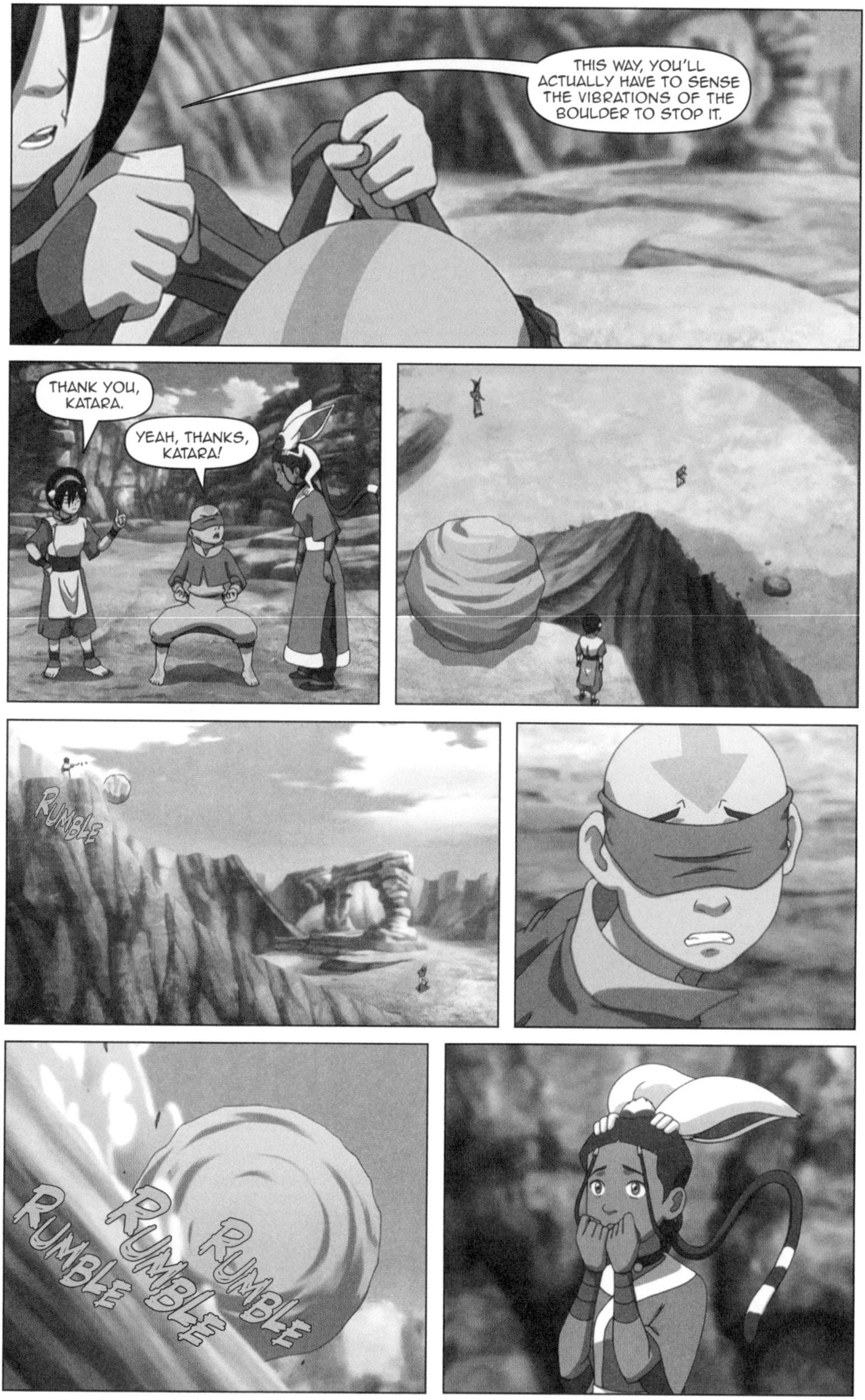
THIS WAY, YOU'LL ACTUALLY HAVE TO SENSE THE VIBRATIONS OF THE BOULDER TO STOP IT.
THANK YOU, KATARA.
YEAH, THANKS, KATARA!
RUMBLE
RUMBLE
RUMBLE
RUMBLE

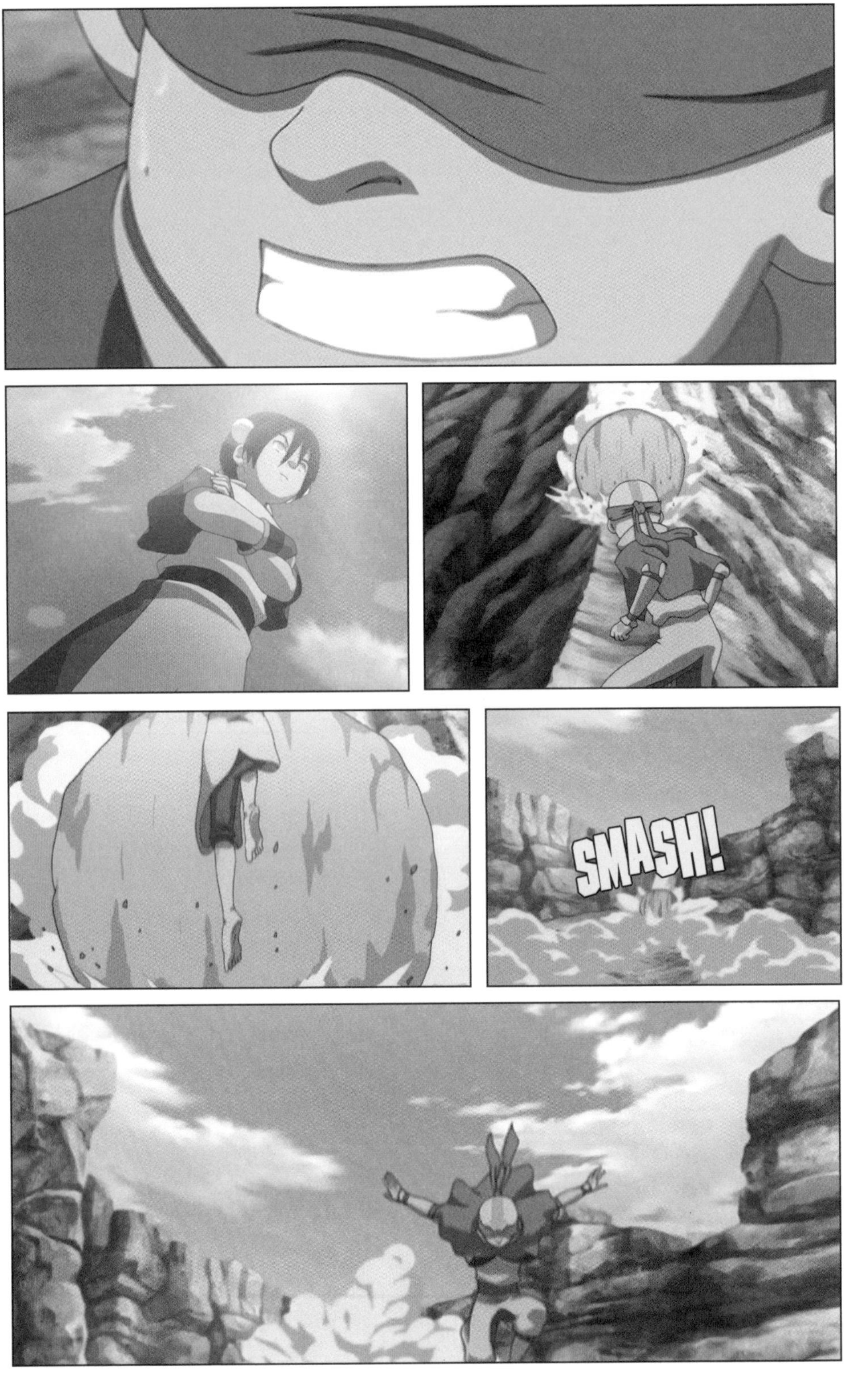
SMASH!

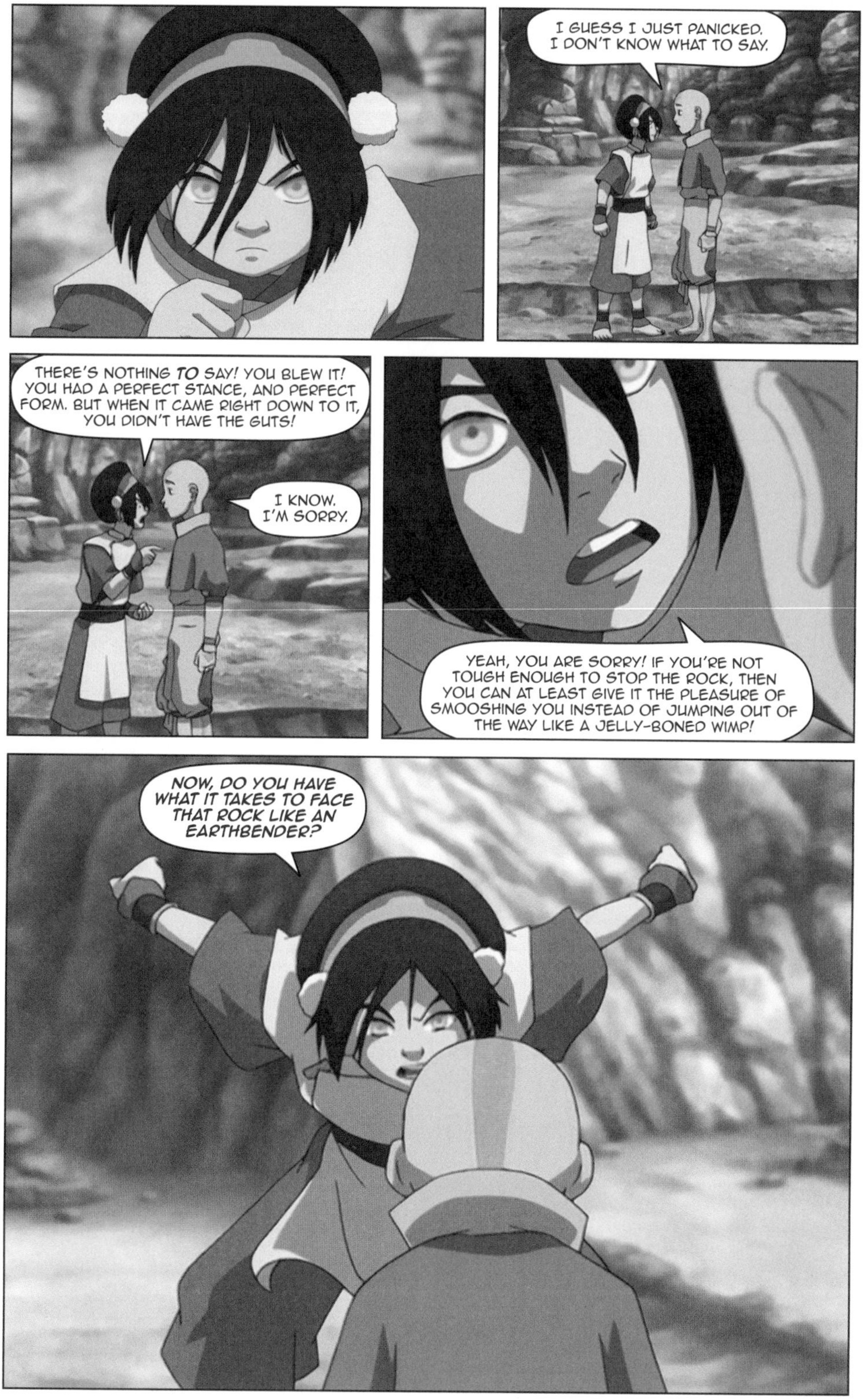
I GUESS I JUST PANICKED. I DON'T KNOW WHAT TO SAY.
THERE'S NOTHING *TO* SAY! YOU BLEW IT! YOU HAD A PERFECT STANCE, AND PERFECT FORM. BUT WHEN IT CAME RIGHT DOWN TO IT, YOU DIDN'T HAVE THE GUTS!
I KNOW. I'M SORRY.
YEAH, YOU ARE SORRY! IF YOU'RE NOT TOUGH ENOUGH TO STOP THE ROCK, THEN YOU CAN AT LEAST GIVE IT THE PLEASURE OF SMOOSHING YOU INSTEAD OF JUMPING OUT OF THE WAY LIKE A JELLY-BONED WIMP!
NOW, DO YOU HAVE WHAT IT TAKES TO FACE THAT ROCK LIKE AN EARTHBENDER?

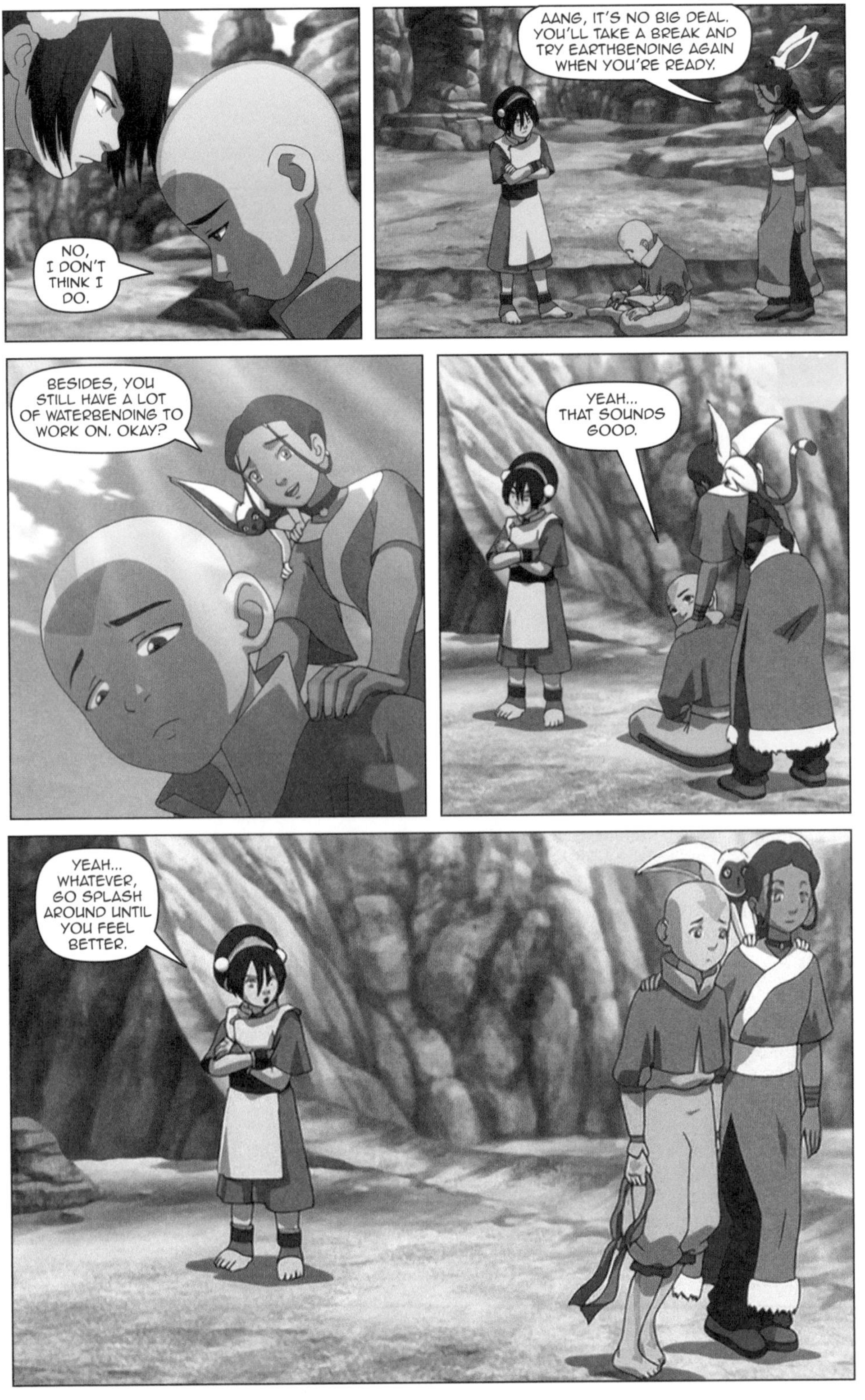
NO, I DON'T THINK I DO.
AANG, IT'S NO BIG DEAL. YOU'LL TAKE A BREAK AND TRY EARTHBENDING AGAIN WHEN YOU'RE READY.
BESIDES, YOU STILL HAVE A LOT OF WATERBENDING TO WORK ON. OKAY?
YEAH... THAT SOUNDS GOOD.
YEAH... WHATEVER, GO SPLASH AROUND UNTIL YOU FEEL BETTER.

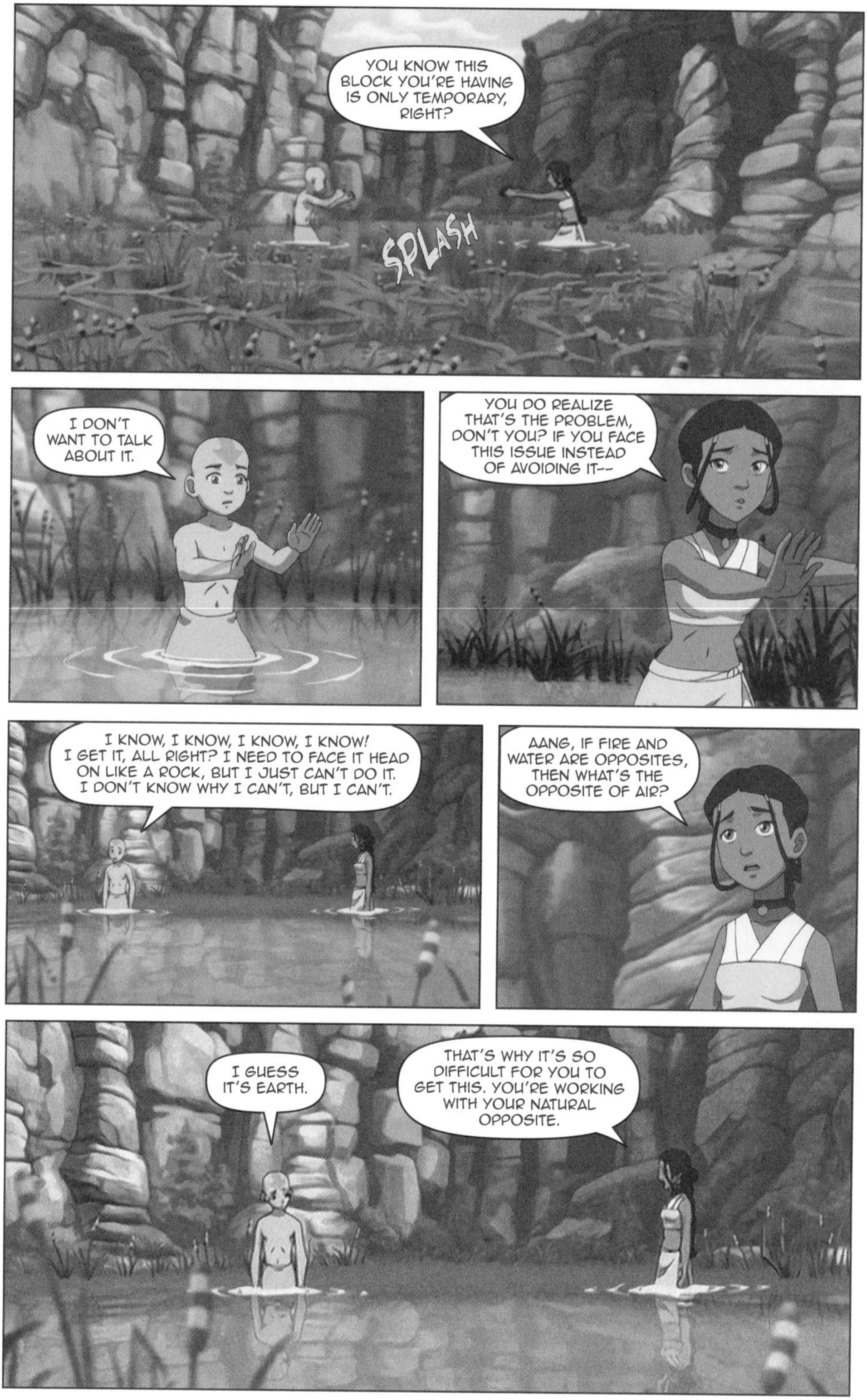
YOU KNOW THIS BLOCK YOU'RE HAVING IS ONLY TEMPORARY, RIGHT?
SPLASH
I DON'T WANT TO TALK ABOUT IT.
YOU DO REALIZE THAT'S THE PROBLEM, DON'T YOU? IF YOU FACE THIS ISSUE INSTEAD OF AVOIDING IT--
I KNOW, I KNOW, I KNOW, I KNOW! I GET IT, ALL RIGHT? I NEED TO FACE IT HEAD ON LIKE A ROCK, BUT I JUST CAN'T DO IT. I DON'T KNOW WHY I CAN'T, BUT I CAN'T.
AANG, IF FIRE AND WATER ARE OPPOSITES, THEN WHAT'S THE OPPOSITE OF AIR?
I GUESS IT'S EARTH.
THAT'S WHY IT'S SO DIFFICULT FOR YOU TO GET THIS. YOU'RE WORKING WITH YOUR NATURAL OPPOSITE.

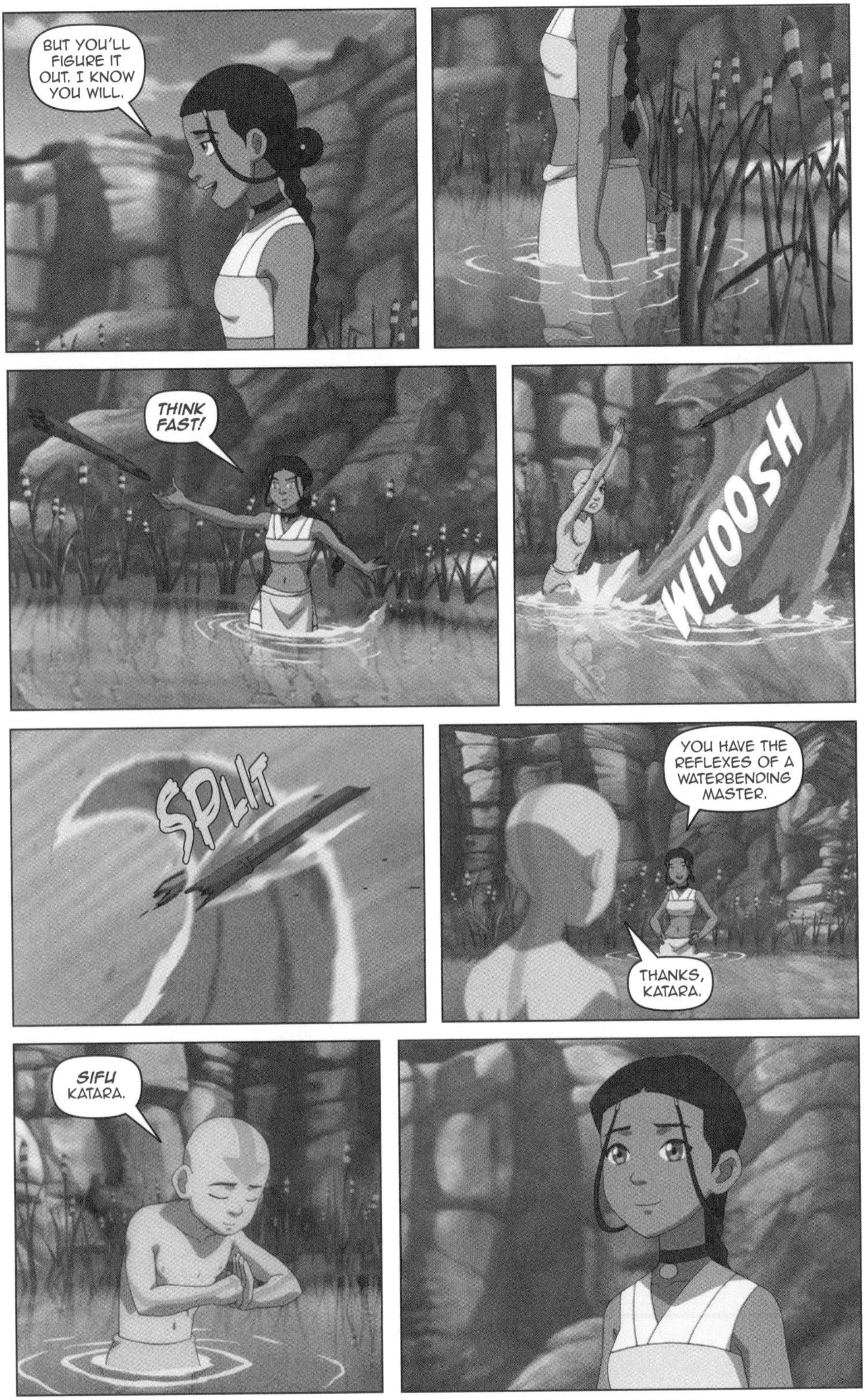
BUT YOU'LL FIGURE IT OUT. I KNOW YOU WILL.
THINK FAST!
WHOOSH
SPLIT
YOU HAVE THE REFLEXES OF A WATERBENDING MASTER.
THANKS, KATARA.
SIFU KATARA.

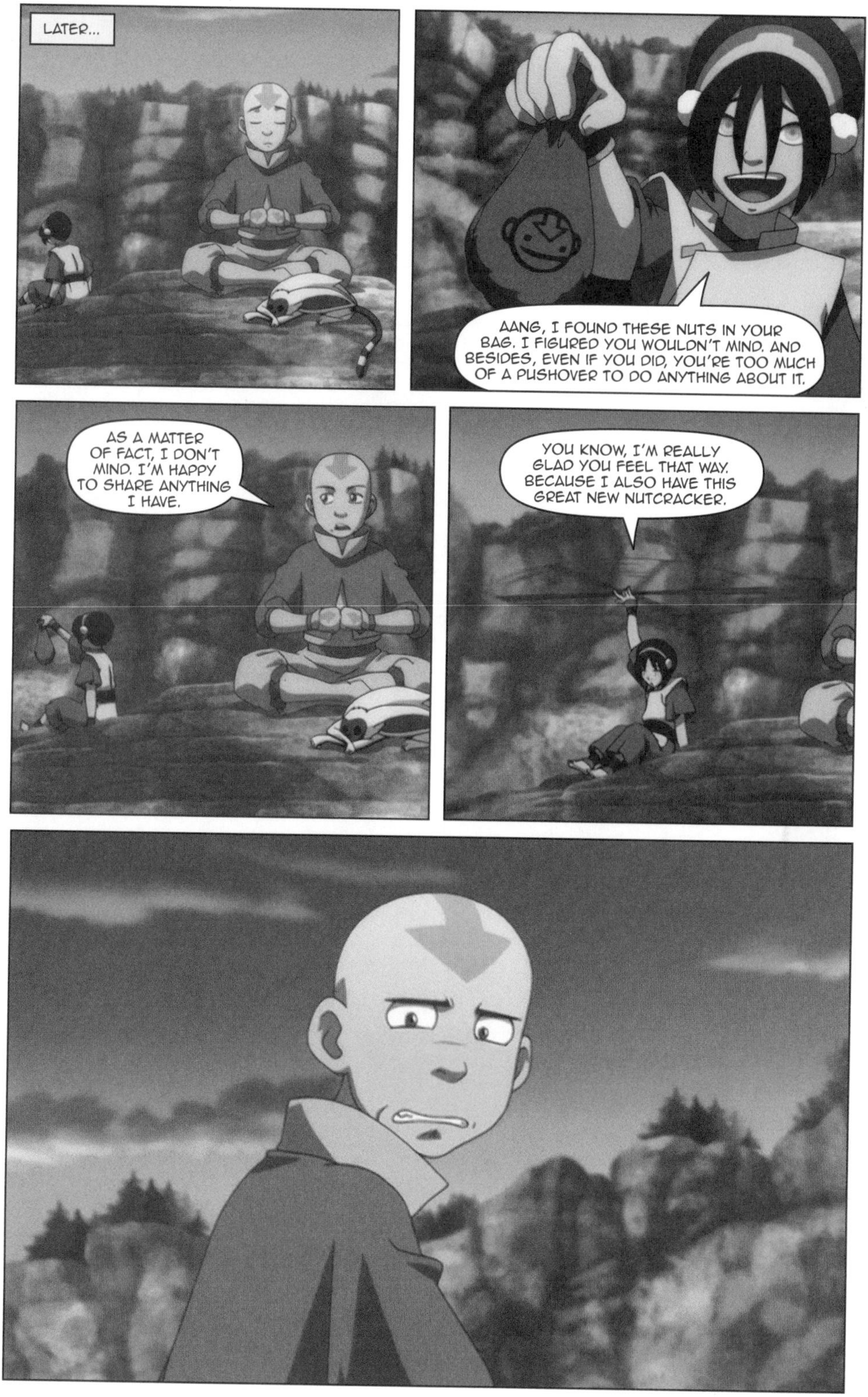
LATER...
AANG, I FOUND THESE NUTS IN YOUR BAG. I FIGURED YOU WOULDN'T MIND. AND BESIDES, EVEN IF YOU DID, YOU'RE TOO MUCH OF A PUSHOVER TO DO ANYTHING ABOUT IT.
AS A MATTER OF FACT, I DON'T MIND. I'M HAPPY TO SHARE ANYTHING I HAVE.
YOU KNOW, I'M REALLY GLAD YOU FEEL THAT WAY. BECAUSE I ALSO HAVE THIS GREAT NEW NUTCRACKER.

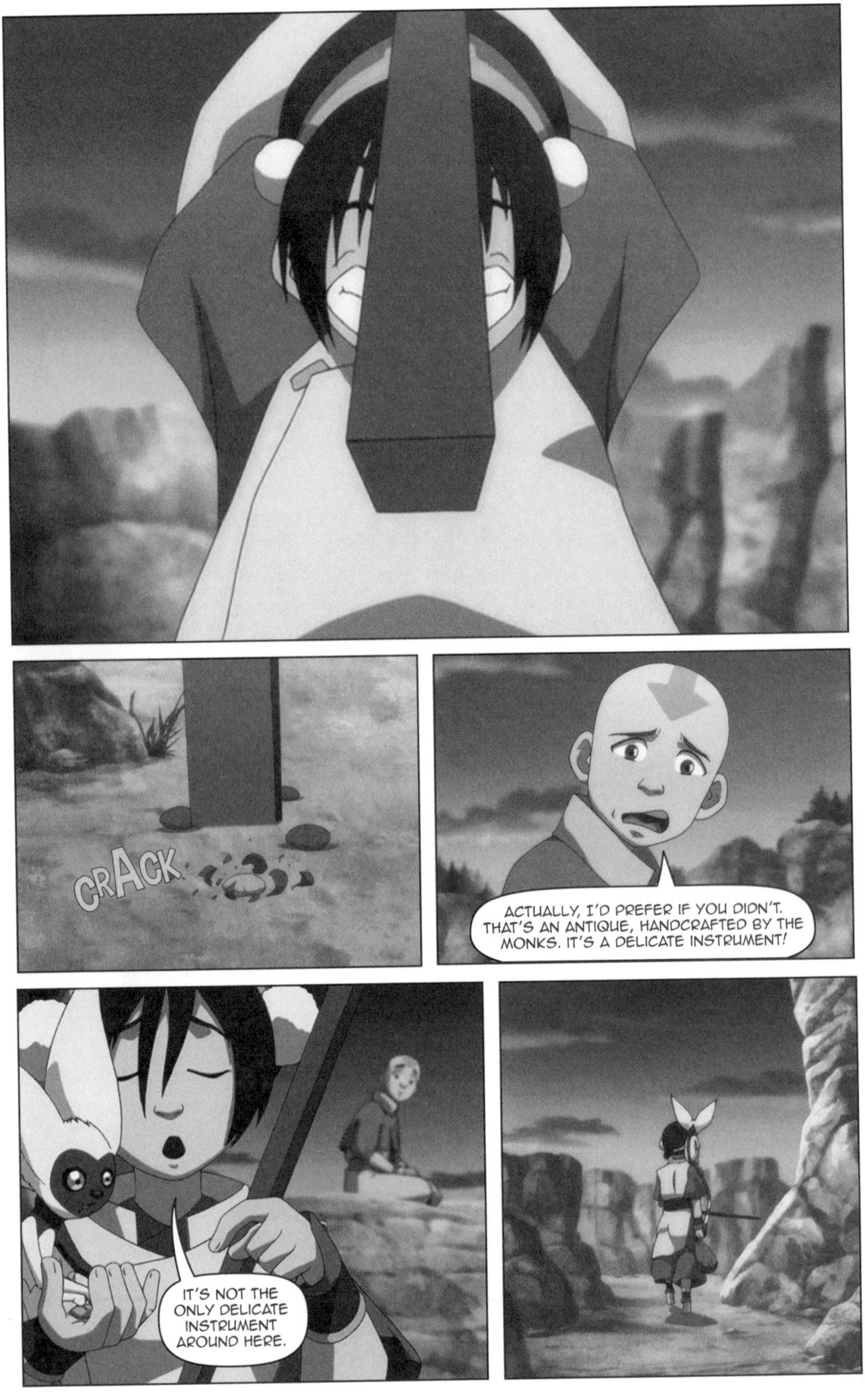
CRACK
ACTUALLY, I'D PREFER IF YOU DIDN'T. THAT'S AN ANTIQUE, HANDCRAFTED BY THE MONKS. IT'S A DELICATE INSTRUMENT!
IT'S NOT THE ONLY DELICATE INSTRUMENT AROUND HERE.

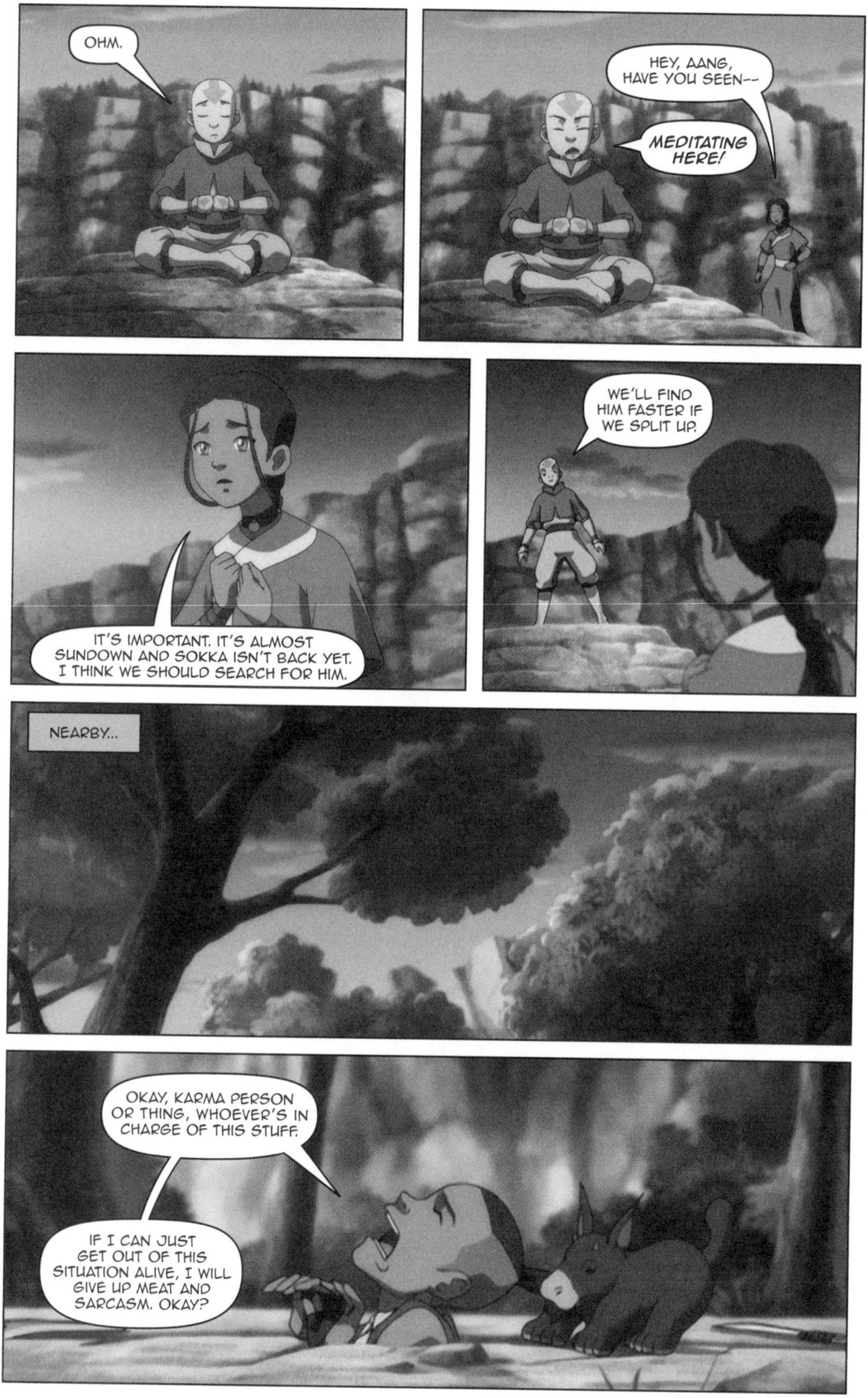
OHM.
HEY, AANG, HAVE YOU SEEN--
MEDITATING HERE!
IT'S IMPORTANT. IT'S ALMOST SUNDOWN AND SOKKA ISN'T BACK YET. I THINK WE SHOULD SEARCH FOR HIM.
WE'LL FIND HIM FASTER IF WE SPLIT UP.
NEARBY...
OKAY, KARMA PERSON OR THING, WHOEVER'S IN CHARGE OF THIS STUFF.
IF I CAN JUST GET OUT OF THIS SITUATION ALIVE, I WILL GIVE UP MEAT AND SARCASM. OKAY?

RRRRIIIIPPPP!

OW!

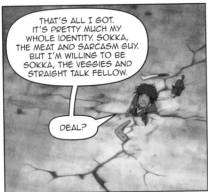

THAT'S ALL I GOT. IT'S PRETTY MUCH MY WHOLE IDENTITY. SOKKA, THE MEAT AND SARCASM GUY. BUT I'M WILLING TO BE SOKKA, THE VEGGIES AND STRAIGHT TALK FELLOW.

DEAL?

AANG!

THANK GOODNESS! HAVE YOU GOT ANY MEAT?

SOKKA! ARE YOU OKAY?

STOP, STOP! YOU'RE GOING TO PULL MY FINGERS OFF AND I DON'T THINK THE REST OF ME IS COMING!

HMMM...I BET I CAN AIRBEND YOU OUT OF HERE.

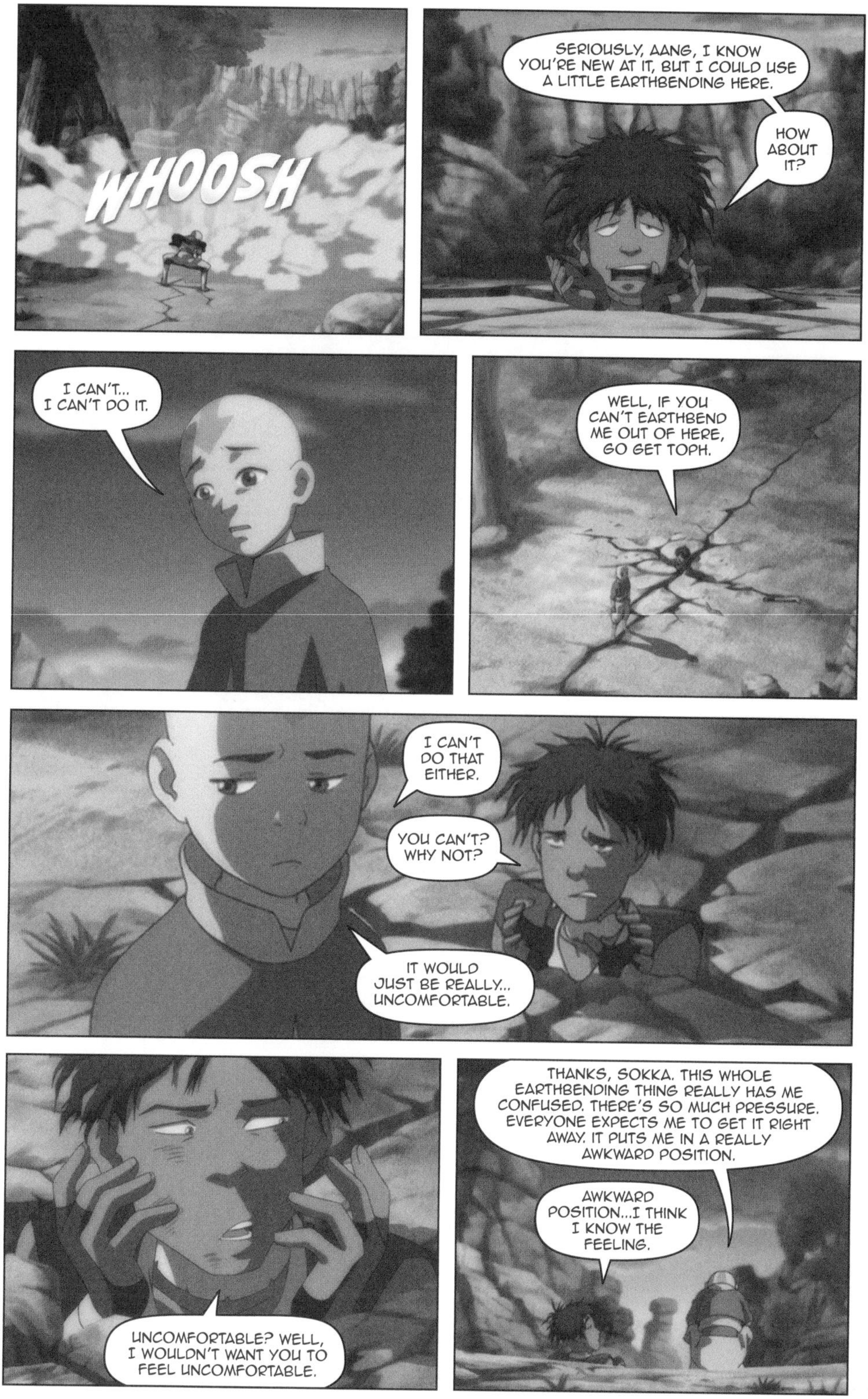
WHOOSH
SERIOUSLY, AANG, I KNOW YOU'RE NEW AT IT, BUT I COULD USE A LITTLE EARTHBENDING HERE.
HOW ABOUT IT?
I CAN'T... I CAN'T DO IT.
WELL, IF YOU CAN'T EARTHBEND ME OUT OF HERE, GO GET TOPH.
I CAN'T DO THAT EITHER.
YOU CAN'T? WHY NOT?
IT WOULD JUST BE REALLY... UNCOMFORTABLE.
UNCOMFORTABLE? WELL, I WOULDN'T WANT YOU TO FEEL UNCOMFORTABLE.
THANKS, SOKKA. THIS WHOLE EARTHBENDING THING REALLY HAS ME CONFUSED. THERE'S SO MUCH PRESSURE. EVERYONE EXPECTS ME TO GET IT RIGHT AWAY. IT PUTS ME IN A REALLY AWKWARD POSITION.
AWKWARD POSITION...I THINK I KNOW THE FEELING.

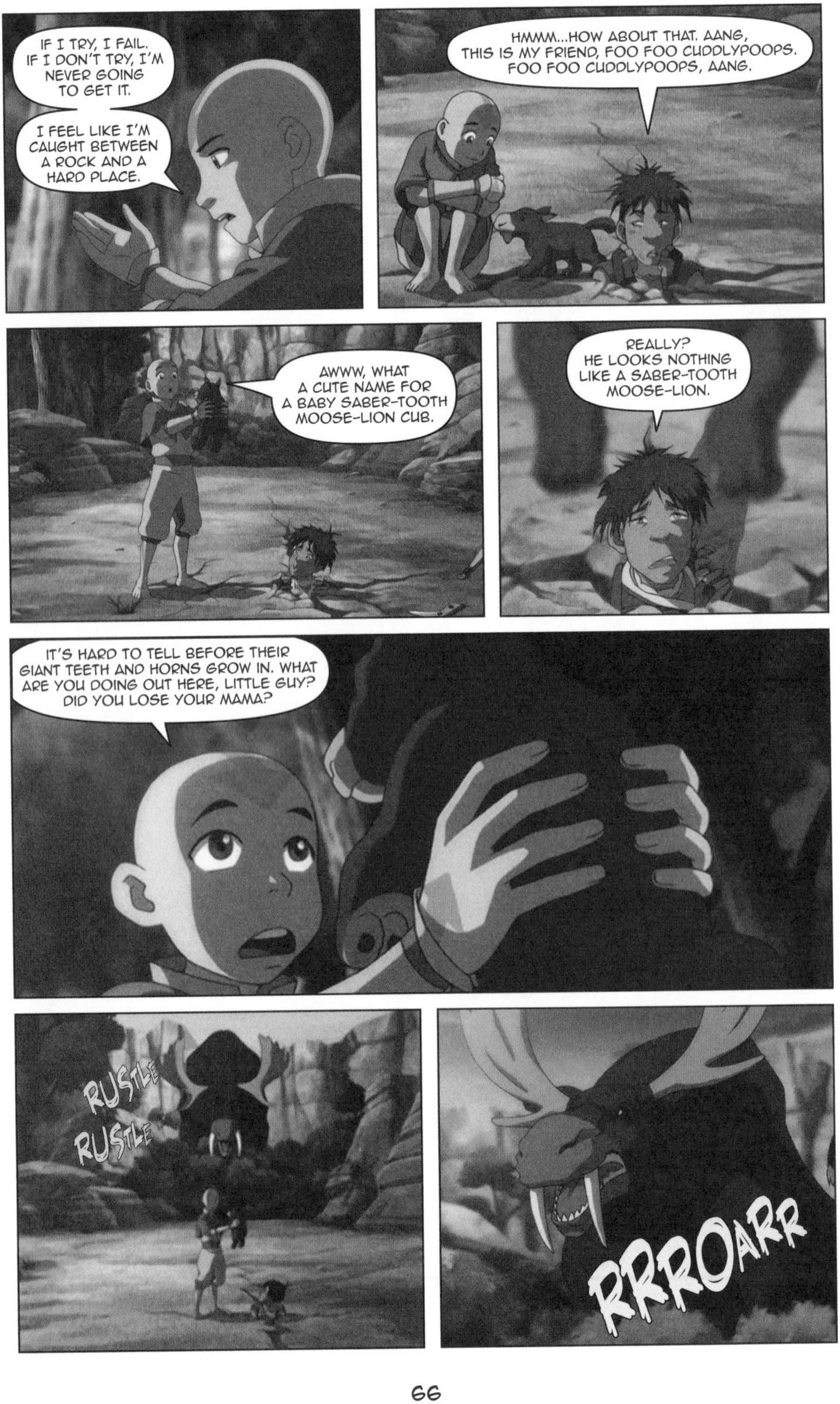
IF I TRY, I FAIL. IF I DON'T TRY, I'M NEVER GOING TO GET IT.
I FEEL LIKE I'M CAUGHT BETWEEN A ROCK AND A HARD PLACE.
HMMM...HOW ABOUT THAT. AANG, THIS IS MY FRIEND, FOO FOO CUDDLYPOOPS. FOO FOO CUDDLYPOOPS, AANG.
AWWW, WHAT A CUTE NAME FOR A BABY SABER-TOOTH MOOSE-LION CUB.
REALLY? HE LOOKS NOTHING LIKE A SABER-TOOTH MOOSE-LION.
IT'S HARD TO TELL BEFORE THEIR GIANT TEETH AND HORNS GROW IN. WHAT ARE YOU DOING OUT HERE, LITTLE GUY? DID YOU LOSE YOUR MAMA?
RUSTLE
RUSTLE
RRROARR

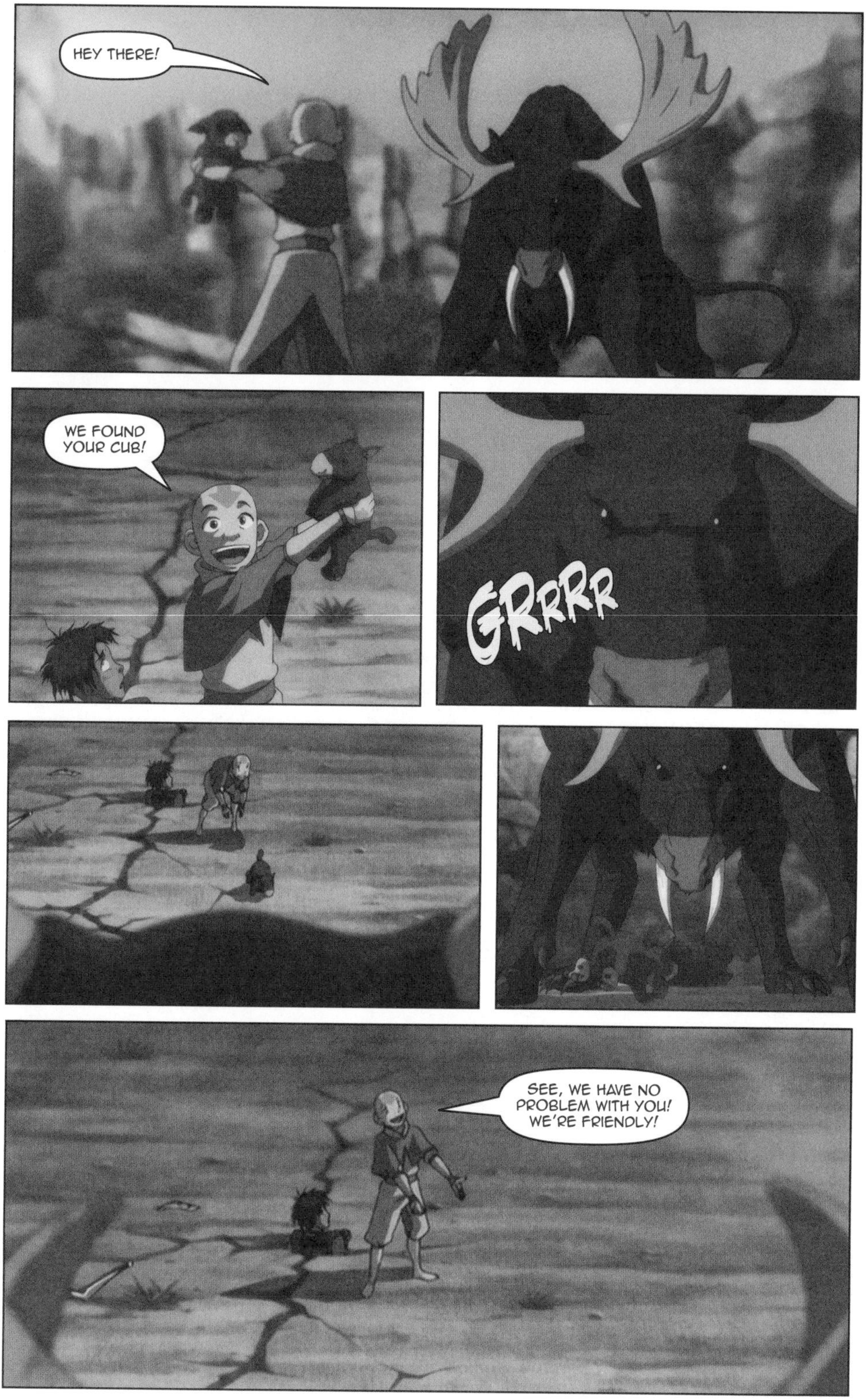
HEY THERE!
WE FOUND YOUR CUB!
GRRRR
SEE, WE HAVE NO PROBLEM WITH YOU! WE'RE FRIENDLY!

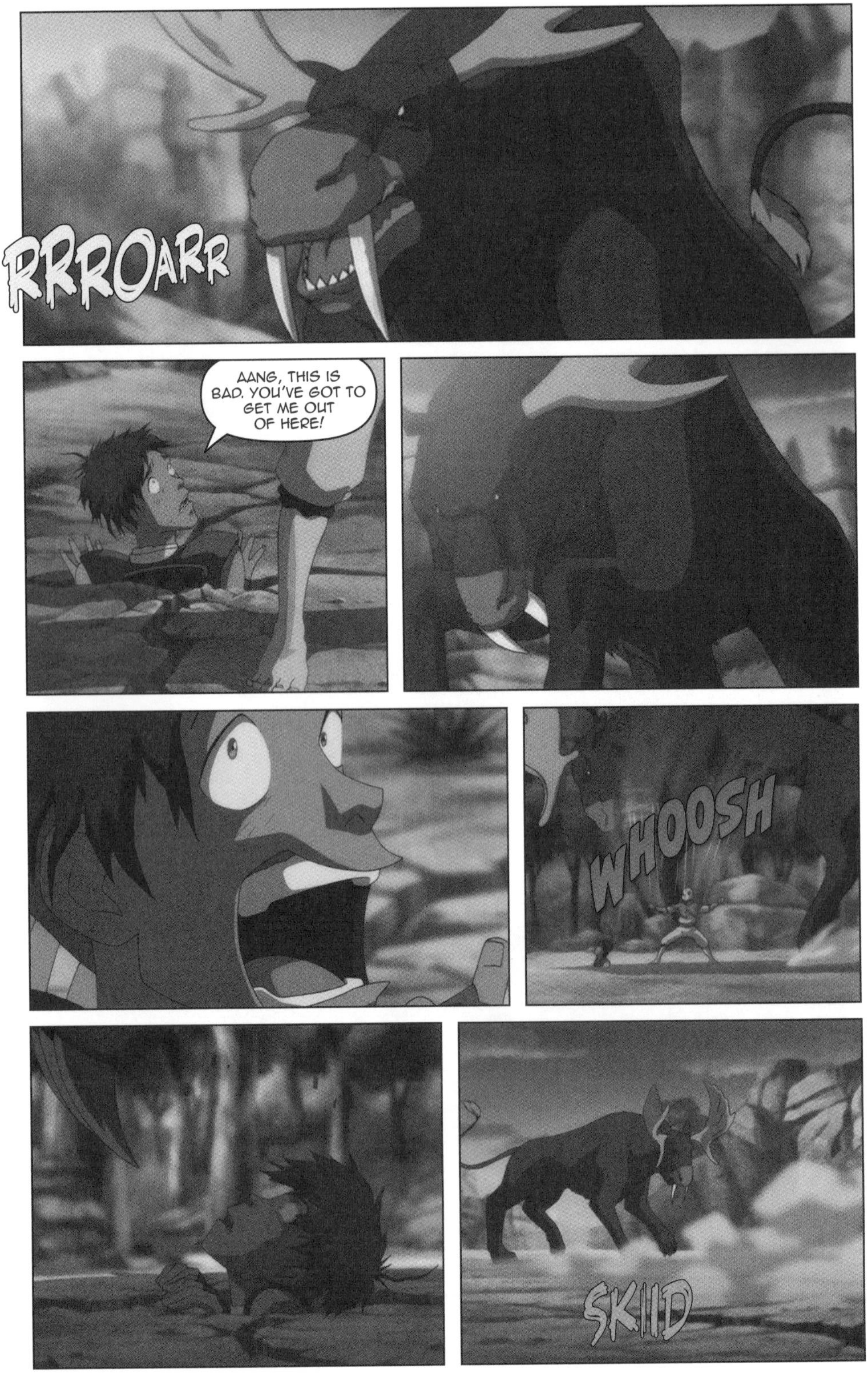
RRROARR
AANG, THIS IS BAD. YOU'VE GOT TO GET ME OUT OF HERE!
WHOOSH
SKIID

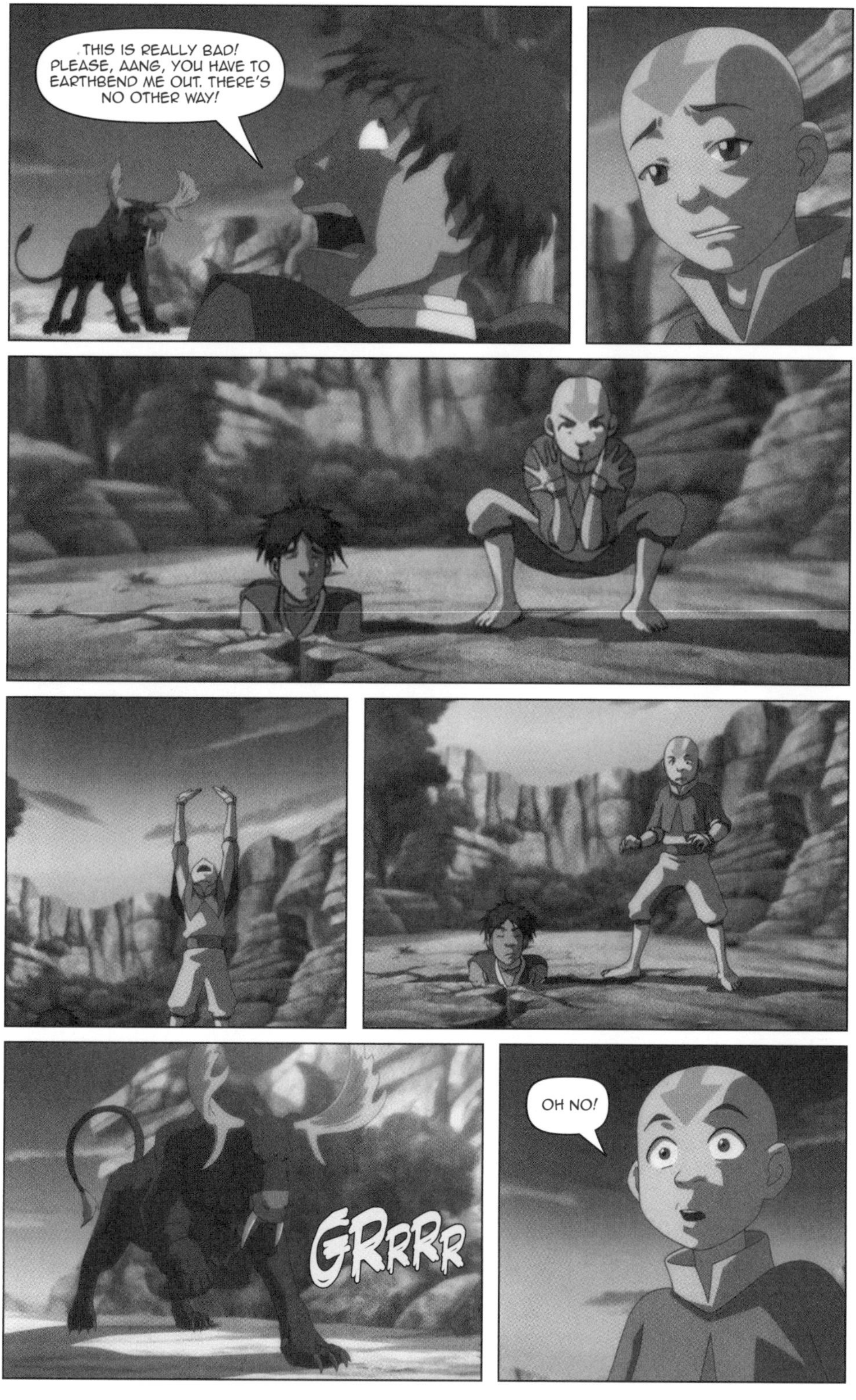
THIS IS REALLY BAD! PLEASE, AANG, YOU HAVE TO EARTHBEND ME OUT. THERE'S NO OTHER WAY!
GRRRR
OH NO!

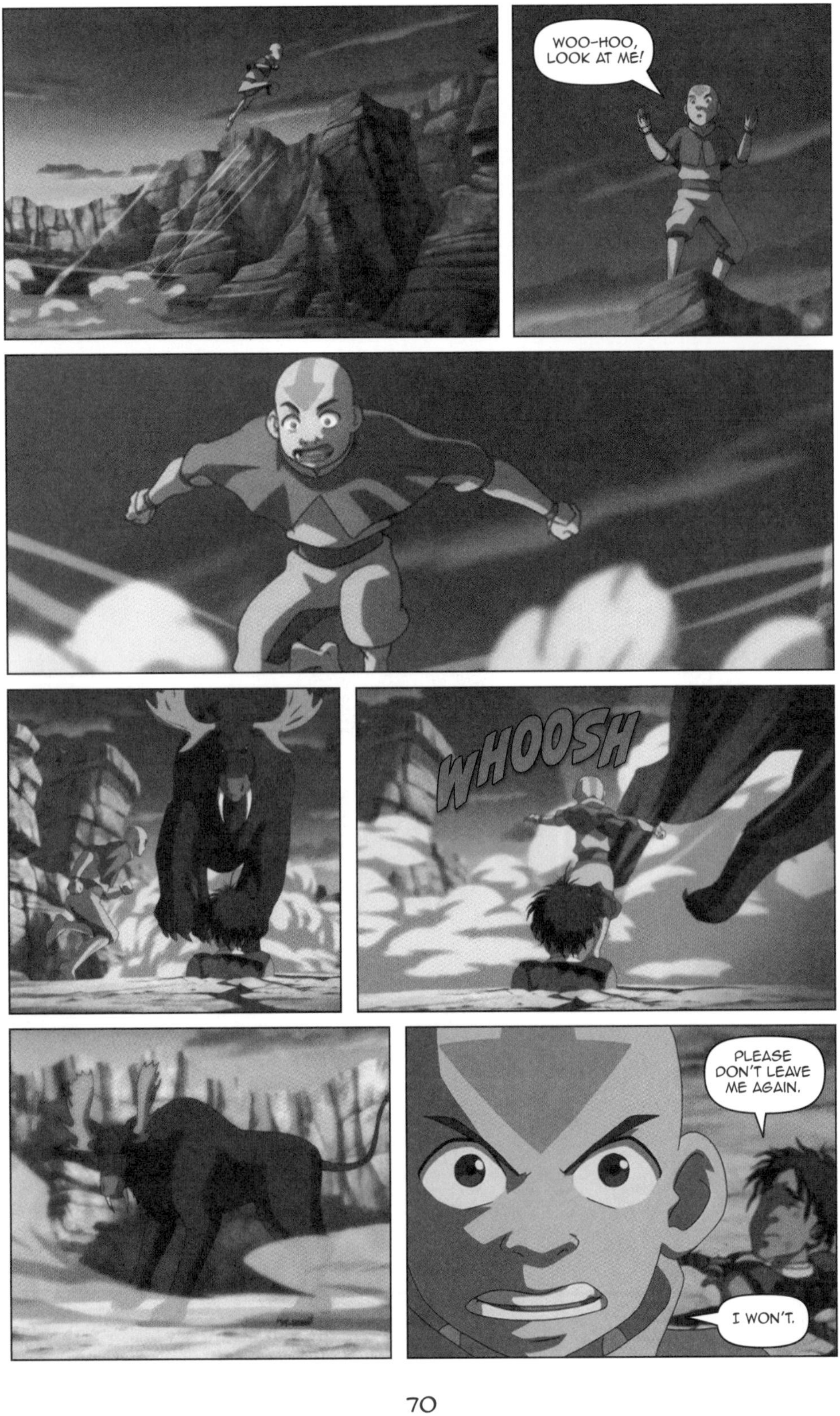
WOO-HOO, LOOK AT ME!
WHOOSH
PLEASE DON'T LEAVE ME AGAIN.
I WON'T.

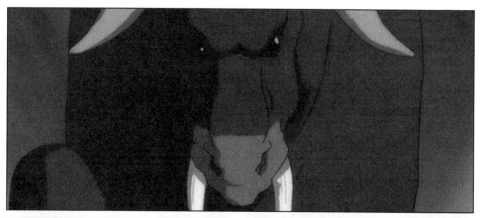

WHAT ARE
YOU DOING
HERE?

JUST
ENJOYING
THE SHOW.

WHAT? YOU
WERE THERE THE
WHOLE TIME?

PRETTY
MUCH.

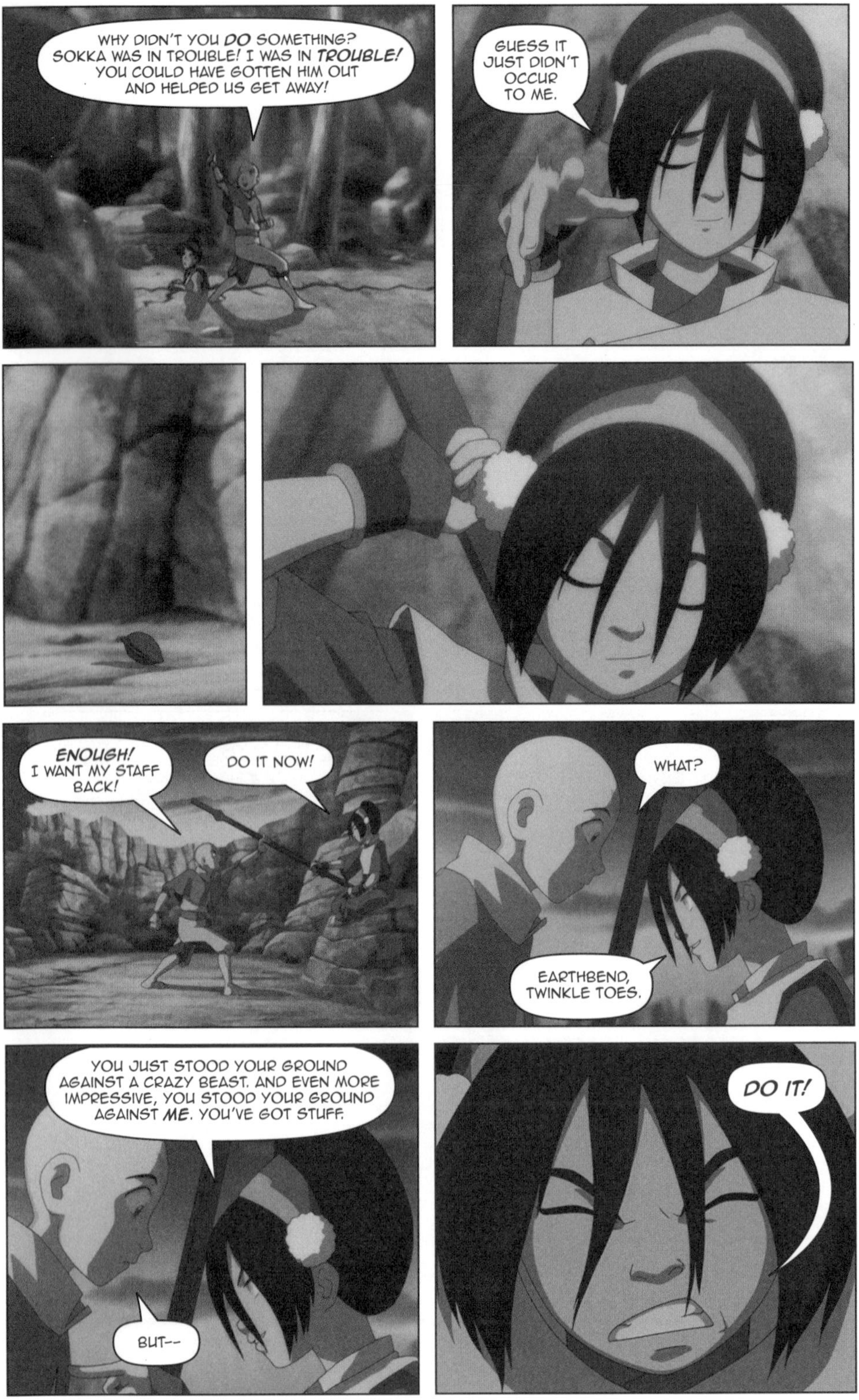
WHY DIDN'T YOU DO SOMETHING? SOKKA WAS IN TROUBLE! I WAS IN TROUBLE! YOU COULD HAVE GOTTEN HIM OUT AND HELPED US GET AWAY!
GUESS IT JUST DIDN'T OCCUR TO ME.
ENOUGH! I WANT MY STAFF BACK!
DO IT NOW!
WHAT?
EARTHBEND, TWINKLE TOES.
YOU JUST STOOD YOUR GROUND AGAINST A CRAZY BEAST. AND EVEN MORE IMPRESSIVE, YOU STOOD YOUR GROUND AGAINST ME. YOU'VE GOT STUFF.
BUT--
DO IT!

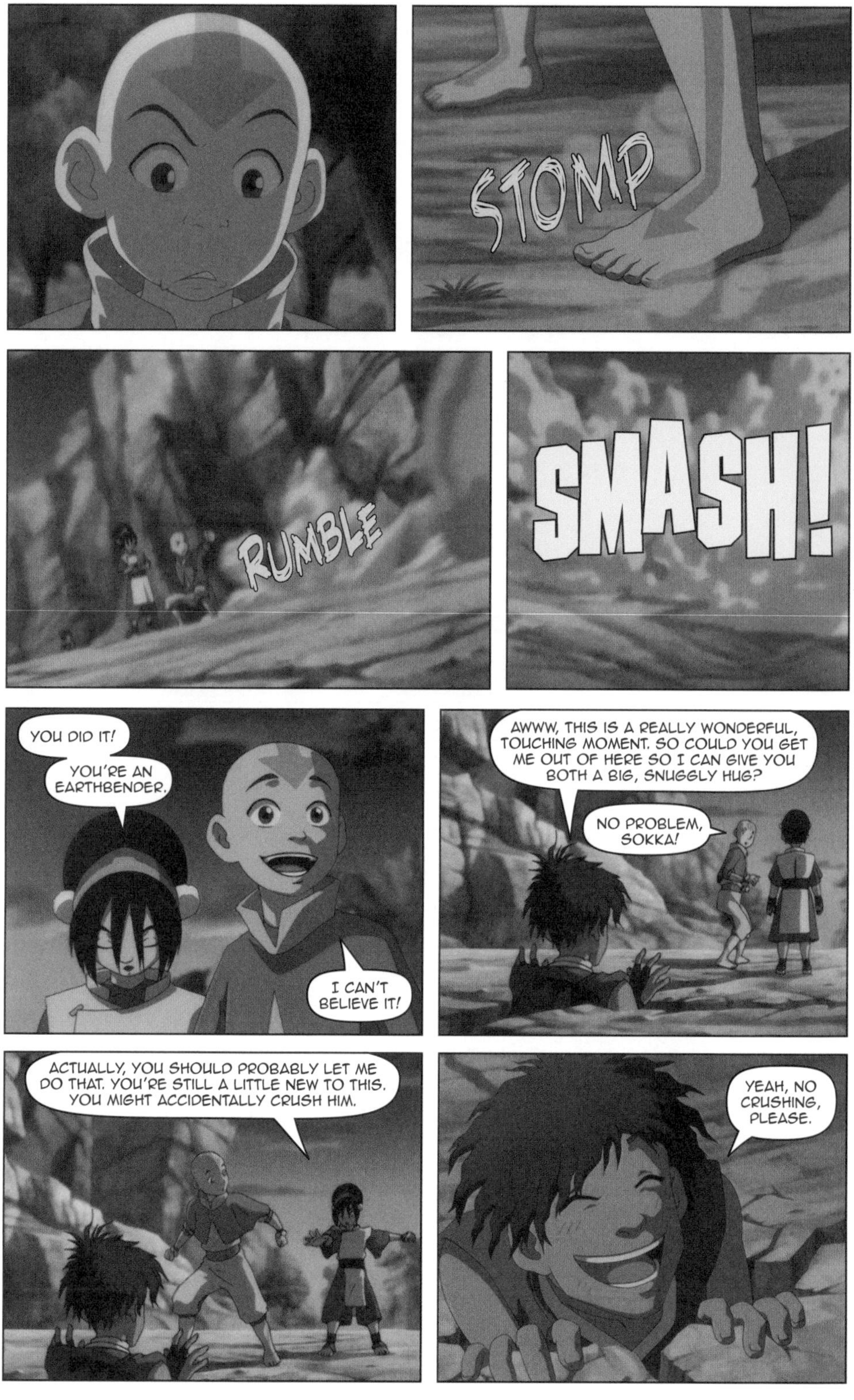
STOMP
RUMBLE
SMASH!
YOU DID IT!
YOU'RE AN EARTHBENDER.
I CAN'T BELIEVE IT!
AWWW, THIS IS A REALLY WONDERFUL, TOUCHING MOMENT. SO COULD YOU GET ME OUT OF HERE SO I CAN GIVE YOU BOTH A BIG, SNUGGLY HUG?
NO PROBLEM, SOKKA!
ACTUALLY, YOU SHOULD PROBABLY LET ME DO THAT. YOU'RE STILL A LITTLE NEW TO THIS. YOU MIGHT ACCIDENTALLY CRUSH HIM.
YEAH, NO CRUSHING, PLEASE.

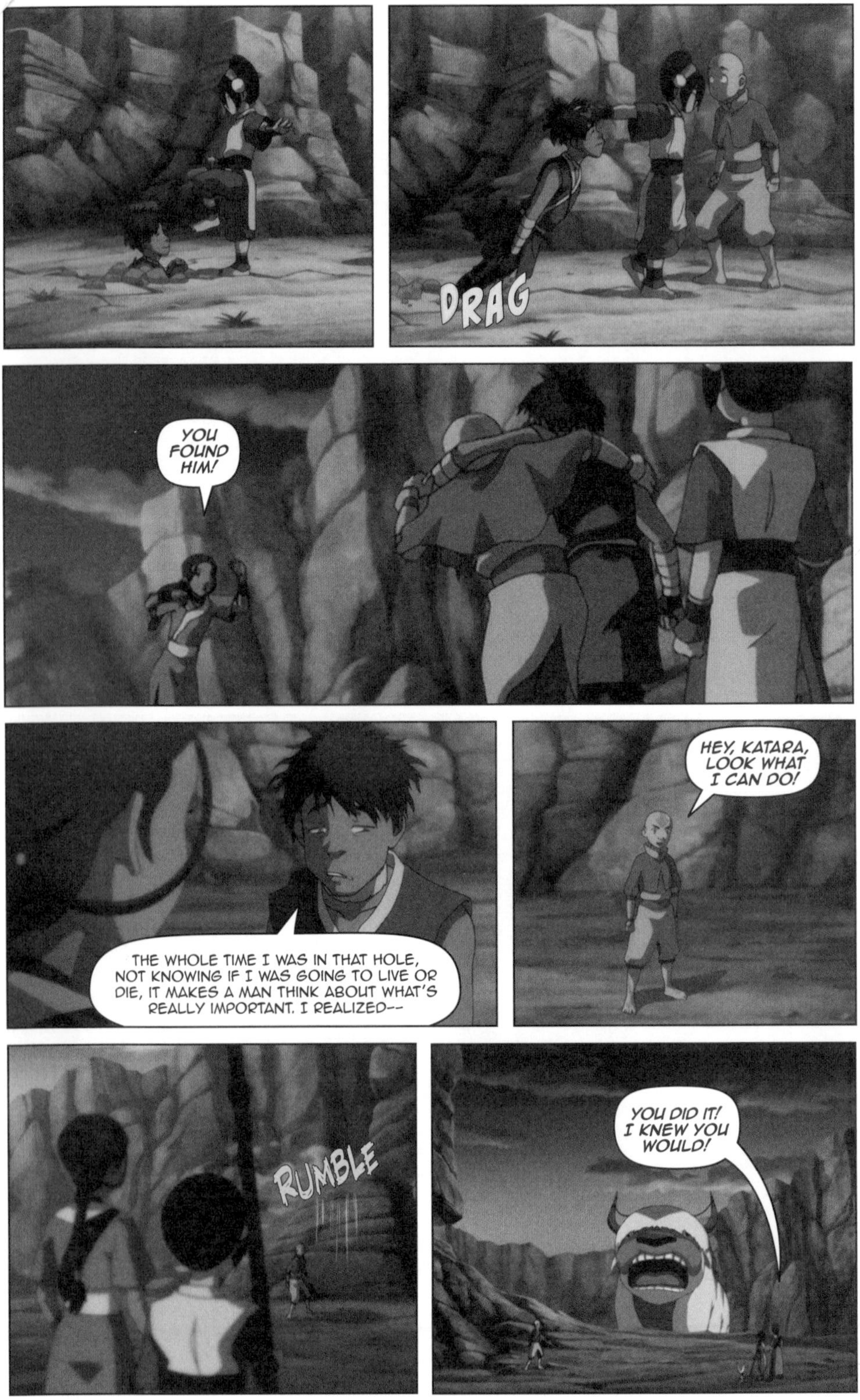
DRAG
YOU FOUND HIM!
THE WHOLE TIME I WAS IN THAT HOLE, NOT KNOWING IF I WAS GOING TO LIVE OR DIE, IT MAKES A MAN THINK ABOUT WHAT'S REALLY IMPORTANT. I REALIZED--
HEY, KATARA, LOOK WHAT I CAN DO!
RUMBLE
YOU DID IT! I KNEW YOU WOULD!

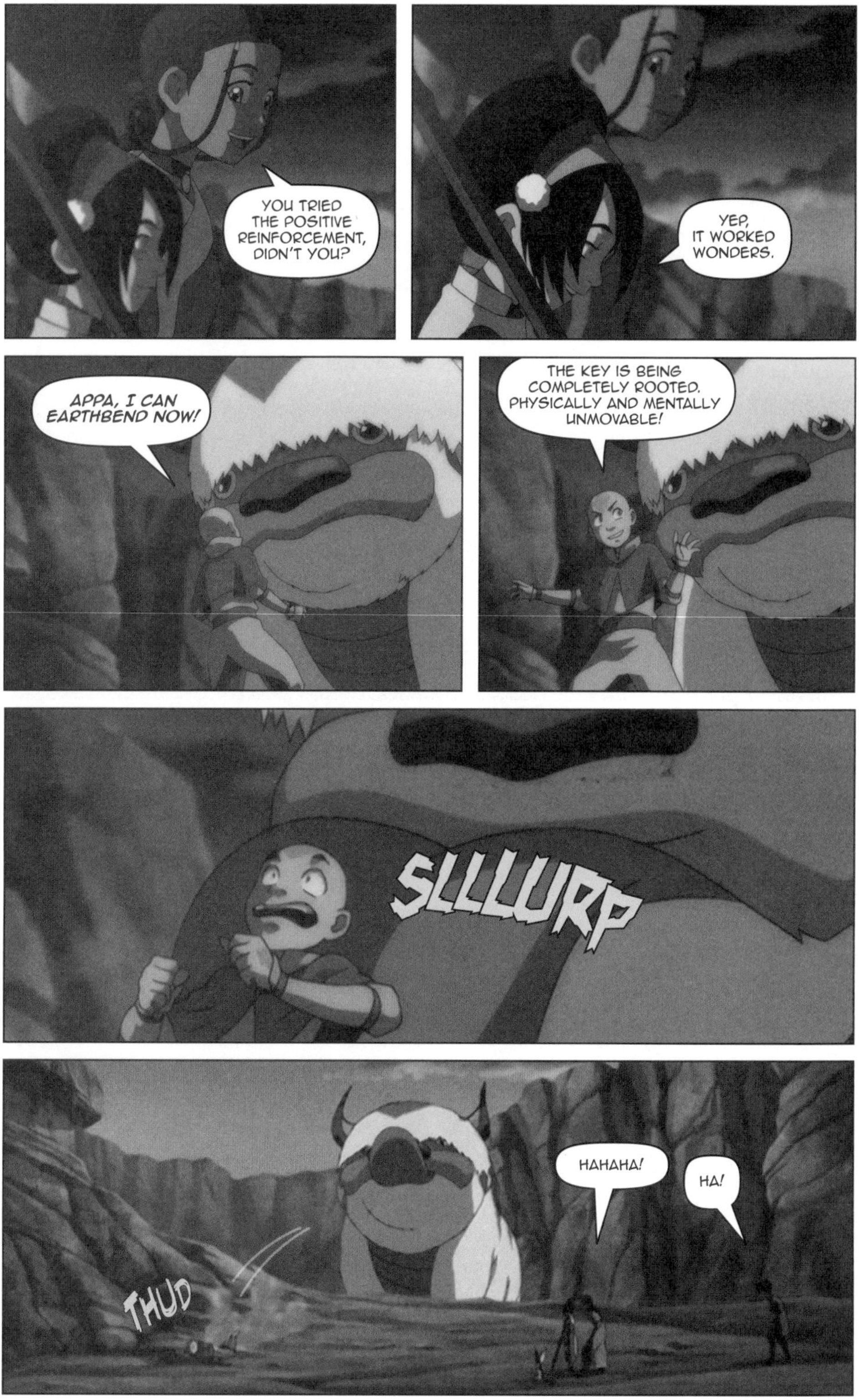
YOU TRIED THE POSITIVE REINFORCEMENT, DIDN'T YOU?
YEP, IT WORKED WONDERS.
APPA, I CAN EARTHBEND NOW!
THE KEY IS BEING COMPLETELY ROOTED. PHYSICALLY AND MENTALLY UNMOVABLE!
SLLLURP
HAHAHA!
HA!
THUD

CREDITS

THE BLIND BANDIT

WRITTEN BY MICHAEL DANTE DIMARTINO

HEAD WRITER
AARON EHASZ

DIRECTED BY ETHAN SPAULDING

CO-EXECUTIVE PRODUCER
AARON EHASZ

BITTER WORK

WRITTEN BY AARON EHASZ

HEAD WRITER
AARON EHASZ

DIRECTED BY ETHAN SPAULDING

CO-EXECUTIVE PRODUCER
AARON EHASZ

nickelodeon

降击神通

AVATAR

THE LAST AIRBENDER.

CREATED BY
MICHAEL DANTE DIMARTINO & BRYAN KONIETZKO